THE NEW ADVENTURES OF
THUNDER
JIM WADE
VOLUME THREE

Edited by - Laurel Copes and Connor MacDonald
Editor in Chief, Pro Se Productions - Tommy Hancock
Director of Corporate Operations- Kristi Morgan
Publisher & Pro Se Productions, LLC - Chief Executive Officer - Fuller Bumpers

Pro Se Productions, LLC
133 1/2 Broad Street
Batesville, AR, 72501
870-834-4022

editorinchief@prose-press.com
www.prose-press.com

"Tomb of Ancient Evil", Copyright © 2018, Frank Schildiner

Cover Art by Mike Fyles
Book Design, Logos, and Additional Graphics by Sean E. Ali
Formatting of E-Book by Antonino lo Iacono and Marzia Marina

New Pulp Logo created by Cari Reese

The New Adventures of Thunder Jim Wade, Volume Three
is a work of the PULP OBSCURA imprint.

PULP OBSCURA is an imprint of Pro Se Productions

THE NEW ADVENTURES OF THUNDER JIM WADE

VOLUME THREE

TOMB OF ANCIENT EVIL

BY

FRANK SCHILDINER

EDITED BY

LAUREL COPES &
CONNOR MACDONALD

PRO SE PRODUCTIONS
2018

THE WORLD WAS dead, a choking, dust-filled, lifeless realm of heat, cold and emptiness. Each step was an exercise in fighting oppression, a rejection of the death that surrounded the band that strode through this terrible land. This was the Kuruk Tagh region of the Gobi desert, a region of the Earth so barren, so lifeless it appeared to be the product of the worst nightmares of a dystopian prophet. Few were willing to venture into this realm where the days were filled with scorching heat and the nights with frigid, bone-jarring cold. Where a mere breeze sent choking sand and dust into your eyes and throat and even the hardiest traveler felt beleaguered by the elements.

But two weeks into the trek, the exploration party was close to their goal. A distant lone, rocky rise was visible in the sand, jutting up from the desert like a singular rotten tooth in the mouth of a madman. The Kuruk Tagh was best known for these rocky mounds. These were the wasted and ruined wrecks of an ancient, majestic mountain range. These hillocks and small mountains were relics of an ancient age clinging to existence as disintegrating sparse ridges in a kingdom empty of life.

According to legend, this former mountain region once held the greatest heights on the planet Earth. They were soaring spires, snow-capped and distant, looking down upon a fertile plain. Scientists, the few willing to venture into this terrible region of the world, believed that millions of years ago, back when the levianthine dinosaurs ruled the world, a series of earthquakes and other disasters struck low these titanic heights. But the men and women who resided near the distant Tarim River basin told, always in whispers, a quite different tale. They spoke of a battle of the gods, a war between the ancient powers of chaos and horror battling the young, protective deities of humanity. This war, whose length varied in the telling each time, threw low these imposing peaks and reduced the bountiful valleys to exhausted plains of dust.

Tristan Twilight, formerly known as Arthur Jones, believed the latter tale in his heart of hearts. Twilight was a believer in many ancient "truths" that others discounted as falsehoods, myths, and tall tales. Born to a family of squires whose income was derived from land and partial interest in a Rothschild's bank, Twilight's family was best known for their desire to rise to a greater social position. His father, made a knight and later a baronet, shipped his sons off to the best schools, where they would receive the bullying education the British public school system was so famous for promoting. As the third son, and one whose intelligence often got him in trouble with teachers, prefects, and his parents, the former Arthur Jones was being groomed for a future in diplomacy or the civil service. He willingly embraced this future, until the day he happened to be persuing the library of a school chum whilst home for the school holidays. Hidden in the back, behind several other leather-bound tomes, was a large book covered in dust with a German title. The title hit him like a fist in the stomach and with a trembling hand he pulled the volume from the shelf and read the words again. *UNAUSSPRECHLICHE KULTEN*. In English the words read as "*Nameless Cults*" or "*Unspeakable Cults*," and the young Arthur Jones was enraptured. Cleaning the cover with a handkerchief, he spent the rest of the night in his guest room, reading the stories of pre-human deities and their followers, many of whom still apparently existed as of the time before the writer killed himself.

This reverential period was finally interrupted when his friend, a charmless pallid boy born to a family with a title dating back to Cnut the Great, knocked and entered the guest room.

"Coming down?" he called. "Oh, sorry, reading again? Not good for the brain at this hour, old thing. What this time?" The young man glanced at the title and visibly shuddered. "German? Why would you read anything by them? You won't find that foreign muck in my library."

The young Twilight smiled and said, "I found it in a book stall. Interesting stuff." And thus began his journey in search of the darker regions of the world. The hidden world became his obsession and all plans of a dull post as a civil servant were forgotten in favor of the study of magic and the lost writing of the pre-human rulers of the Earth. He studied under Crowley and Mathers before moving to the continent, Asia, and even regions of Africa and South America to learn from elderly masters of lost traditions. Changing his name to Tristan Twilight, he was largely discounted as a nutter with a fascination for mythical worlds, ignored or scoffed at by the academic world. His lack of interest in publicity or notoriety, unlike that of Crowley, earned him a level of respect from some and his family, while keeping their distance socially, supported his odd mania financially.

Now, thirty years since first reading that poor copy of *Nameless Cults*, Twilight was about to retire to a small country estate owned by his family. There he would have continued his studies and written articles and his unnamed grand work on the darker world. But one of his few followers, Phillip Brand, who was better known as Lord Lister, presented him with the recently uncovered rubbings of the Pnakotic Fragments, ones believed destroyed when they were first uncovered. These fragments spoke of a lost tomb, the true rulers of the world and how they waited, sleeping. Twilight knew this was the culmination of his work, the proof he needed as to the lost worlds of ancient mankind. Finding this mythical crypt became his mania, until the day he and Lord Lister hired their train of guides and headed off into the deep deserts of the Gobi.

Now the location was in sight, a mere day's journey by camel. Though determined to achieve his goal, Twilight was an experienced explorer in the darker districts of the world. They stopped for the night and broke camp before dawn, arriving at the prominent lone ridge before the blinding heat of the day struck them full-force.

The once majestic mountain was a mere ridge now, approximately two hundred yards around and five hundred or so feet high. It was a craggy sand covered pile, a ruined relic of ancient days, a wrecked monument to a once mighty range that dominated the world. There was a forlorn quality to this remnant of geologic greatness, a crumbling edifice of a time before mankind ruled the world.

A disquieting sensation, an inner trepidation entered every member of the party without apparent reason. The bearers and guides, normally a cheerful band despite the harsh conditions, fell strangely quiet. They spoke in hushed tones, their guttural Chinese/Mongolian patois unrecognizable to all ears other than those of this region. The Europeans, Twilight and his follower Lord Lister, shivered despite the extreme heat, having slept poorly, and broke out in cold sweats as they approached the hillock. Twilight's dreams were filled with shadowy terrors, unseen monstrosities of the id that caused him to wake and suppress screams of fright several times through the night.

Camp was set in a cauldron-shaped valley a short distance from the rocky mound. The bearers set up the tents, keeping their temporary dwellings as far from the ridge and stonily refused to approach any closer. Twilight attempted to persuade, trick and even threaten these hearty desert dwellers, without any success. They supplied several canteens of water and a long length of heavy rope, but returned to their tents, speaking in hushed muttering tones. Their eyes were suspicious and angry, their discomfort almost a physical force that struck the two Englishmen.

Twilight and Lister, usually forceful types towards those they believed to be below their social position, found themselves sympathizing with the rough bearers. There was something wrong about this location, not just the inner superstition caused by ancient tales. Their reaction was a deeper, inner fear-based response, the ancient imperative of "fight or flight" built into all sentient beings from the time of their creation. Although quite sophisticated beings, all of the humans present felt an almost unbearable desire to flee from this ancient elevation. Only the strong minds of the bearers and the inner determination of the two Europeans were able to overcome this terrible sensation.

Despite the short distance, it took nearly an hour for Twilight and Lister to approach the edge of the promontory. The shifting sands and sudden rocky dips made the terrain treacherous unless they crossed the land with the uppermost care. Standing in a small patch of shade, the two men stared up at the hillock, cognizant that the feeling of unease was even stronger at this time.

Pulling out his diary, Twilight leafed through the yellowing pages until he reached a particular passage he copied with extreme care months prior to this expedition. Reading and translating the words again, he looked up at Lister, leaning against a large boulder and sipping from a canteen. Lister was a tall man with a long nose and a weak chin. His eyes were large and perpetually looked both watery and surprised and his pencil mustache was dark and looked as if it was a centipede asleep across his upper lip. Lister was a surprisingly intelligent man, well-read and possessing a willingness and desire to expand his learning. As a wealthy noble, he was able to indulge his scholarly desires, which, in Lord Lister's case, were the true origins of man. Lister did not believe that life began with simple hunter-gatherer tribes in Africa and the Near East; instead he held to the theories of a greater history of mankind. He spent much of his ever-growing fortune on this subject, buying ancient tomes and maps in an attempt to discover the "truth." But this also demonstrated his greatest failing: credulity. The man was willing to attempt to follow any crack-brained theory on his pet subject, causing him to follow Twilight across the world in search of answers to the true origins of humanity.

Twilight reread the passage five more times, ensuring that the translation was exactly the same on each occasion. He was a man of medium height with a fleshy body that was formerly taut and muscular. A lover of his indulgences, Twilight looked older than his years, all the more so since losing all of his hair after a bout of malaria on a trip to Peru in search of an ancient temple. But it was his eyes that caused people to stare at him and miss his apparent bacchanalian caused physical ruination. They were large and violet in color, enticing and hypnotic. A fierce intelligence lay behind those prominent orbs, a desire to learn the secrets lost to mankind and be the one true magus in the world. Though there was still a great deal of the charlatan in his actions, these were mere playacting to hide his greater mission. From his readings, the great wielders of mystic might acted as the Priest Kings of the ancient world. These men and women were the true gods of the world, protectors, rulers and destroyers. They were granted the right to indulge their appetites in return for the use of their eldritch wisdom in defense of the world. That was what Twilight, the former Arthur Jones, gleaned from *UNAUSSPRECHLICHE KULTEN* all those years ago. The hidden cults of the world would follow his lead once he earned the true power of the ancients. The Earth would change for the better, and a new age would be ushered into the world.

"According to my information, we need to find a boulder that possesses a large handprint on its face. When pushed, it will move and reveal an entry into the depths of the tomb. If we work diligently, we should find this within the week," Twilight explained and pulled out two soft bristled brushes from his pack.

"A handprint you say?" Lister said, wiping his brow with a red handkerchief.

Twilight nodded, having known this would be a difficult portion of the journey. Lister, while interested in ancient world theories, never got his hands dirty in the studies. With the bearers shunning this location, Twilight knew he would require the willing aid of this man.

"I realize this will be dirty and difficult. But I believe with fast and efficient work, we will find the etching within the week," Twilight explained, showing the brushes.

"But—" Lister protested, looking surprised.

Twilight extended the brush. "It is the most essential step, my friend. We must put aside our desire to avoid such labor and find this crypt!"

"But—" Lister protested again, stepping forward and ignoring the extended brushes.

Twilight thrust the brushes forward. "We can do this, my friend! Please don't walk away when we are so close!"

"But," Lister echoed and pointed over Twilight's shoulder, "isn't that a hand-shaped print on that rock over there, Twilight? I mean, we can brush and brush if I'm wrong, but that looks like a bally big paw to my eyes!"

Twilight wanted to scream in annoyance and frustration. There were times when Lister's upper-class means of expressing himself were deeply frustrating. The man, like many of such upbringing, appeared barely able to express a thought without forcing one to wait an interminable amount of time. This led many to view him as a fool, a great mistake. Lord Lister was no man's fool, despite his credulity on the secrets of the universe. And he did fairly worship Twilight. Which was why England's most infamous magus didn't scream or strike the man. Instead, he merely smiled and clapped Lister on the shoulder in a comradely fashion.

"Well done, well done!" Twilight bellowed and stepped up to the stone. The handprint was larger, far longer and wider that a normal man's hand. This was the palm print of a giant, a being of ancient days capable of rending an enemy in pieces with little to no effort. There were many tales of such beings, men whose giant stature, mighty thews, and skills placed them above the common stock of humanity. Twilight dreamed of these beings long before he discovered the hidden path of the world, the dark underside that mankind pretended did not exist.

"Just luck, don't you know," Lister replied, blushing slightly at the praise. "Happened to see the bally big paw in the light as we were talking, don't you know. How does that get us inside?"

Twilight tapped his notes with a finger. "Apparently, we lay our hand on the engraving and it will move with ease. That was how others appeared to have entered the depths of the tomb of the ancients." He paused a moment and decided to give his follower something that would make him feel important. "Place your hand on the print, my friend. You found it. This should be your honor."

Lister started in surprise and stared at Twilight with wide, watery eyes. He looked about to sob but pulled himself together and reached for the print. He paused a few inches from the imprint and asked, "Is it safe? I won't lose a hand or some such?"

Twilight suppressed an urge to strike the man or scream and merely breathed in deeply, coughed from the dust he inhaled, and shook his head. "There was never any word of any traps or pitfalls in all my research."

The English nobleman brightened and smiled, his gapped and jagged teeth shining brightly in the harsh desert sunlight. "Ah! Well that's all right then!" he said, and placed his palm on the etching.

And nothing happened. The stone remained fixed in place and no amount of pushing or pulling budged the titanic boulder so much as an inch. Lister stepped away and wiped his head again, looking expectantly at Twilight. He clearly was waiting for a miracle but did not wish to suggest such an act to his mentor.

Twilight frowned, wondering if there was some reason Lister's attempt failed. Was the ancient mechanism destroyed by the sands of time? That was the explanation he could use if they could not discover the means into the ancient tomb. But in his heart of hearts, he hoped the device would work. That would be clear proof to all, Lister being the first, that he was a being beyond humanity.

Reaching out, Twilight placed his hand on the stone. The carving, though scratched into an ancient stone edifice, felt soft, almost spongy under his touch. With a slight movement of his arm, the stone slid back, almost weightless in his hand. And then, with a puff of dust, appeared a large round opening in the wall of the ridge. The appearance was startling, to say the least. The opening in a set of ancient rocks should have caused a rumbling, a small tremor of motion at their feet. But there was nothing, no motion in the rock wall, no vibrations in the slightest. All that resulted was a mere puff of dust, a displacement of the sands that lay upon this elder geologic foundation.

"We've found the tomb of the ancients," Lister whispered, his face filled with awe and a trace of fear.

"Yes, I have," Twilight stated, subtly correcting his follower. He would be the one who lead this step into history, nobody else. His work would be known, and Lister would be merely known as a follower, an underling with some ready capital. This was the way things were meant to be. People remembered Howard Carter when he discovered a minor Kinglet; few knew of Carnarvon, his patron. The same would occur when the crypt which once housed mankind's masters was unearthed and explored.

Lighting their lanterns and checking their supplies again, Twilight, followed by Lister, cautiously stepped into the cave. They didn't speak and stepped with a tentative, almost reverent tread. The floor and walls were made of smooth, almost glassine surface that was as easy to walk upon as a paved road. The walkway possessed a slight decline and after one hundred or so yards, began to turn sharply to the left. It was mere moments later that both men realized the corridor they were traversing was spiraling downward, moving deeper and deeper into the surface of the earth.

But it was the air that surprised both explorers the most of all. For weeks they learned of the many scents of the deep Gobi Desert, a stench filled with dust, small animals and an arid quality one only experienced in the dustbowls of the world. But this scent was far different, a unique harsh smell devoid of even the parsimonious life that was the Gobi. The air felt lifeless, as if the very energy was torn from the invisible molecules and leaving behind a harsh, almost burning gas that barely supplied life. This forced Twilight and Lister to move at a far slower pace, slightly faster than a crawl. The very harshness of the air as well as the continued serpentine depths they were forced to traverse left both men both breathless and silent when they finally reached a small chamber at the bottom.

The room was a small box-shaped compartment with the same smooth walls, untouched by dust. But the floor, also made of the same material, appeared to glitter in several places from the light of their lanterns. The largest glow came from the center of the room, a harsh white reflection that caused both men to wince from the glare. Twilight stepped closer, shielding his lantern with a hand to study the source. A moment later he started, shocked by his realization.

"It's…it's a…jewel…" he whispered, staring at the three-foot circle before his feet. The shimmer was caused by thousands of facets built into a gem that was easily as large as a man's torso. The jewel was clear, and the crystalline composition caused each beam of light to glitter with prismatic power, hiding the depth of the enormous object. With a shaking hand, Twilight reached out and touched the hard, yet warm surface.

The gem's luminescence seemed to grow after his light caress, causing him to withdraw his hand in fright. The room's walls also began to glow lightly, throwing a pale, farinaceous illumination in the box-shaped space. Twilight stepped back, feeling a light vibration through the soles of his feet. He was frozen in place, sensing the decisive moment of his lifelong quest had come to fruition. Yet his anxiety grew with each second, a literal moment of truth in his life.

Abruptly, yet silently, the nearby wall slid aside and a monstrous jewel slid into view. The crystal was a pale yellow in color and appeared to pulse with a gold energy that sent a soft glow about the room. Twilight and Lister found the rays emitting from this luminescence relaxing them, causing their tensed, wire-tight muscles to unknot slowly. A gentle smile appeared on both of their faces, allowing them to stare at the magnificent jewel.

Part of Twilight's mind rebelled against this physical and emotional transformation, sensing a manipulative impropriety behind their reactions. He struggled internally, his skin suddenly shivering as he watched his follower drop to his knees in apparent supplication. Twilight fought silently, rejecting the inner demand to stare in beatific satisfaction at the crystalline structure that appeared to mandate their subservience.

The jewel slowly began to vanish, the facets each vanishing and revealing a dark, gaping open sarcophagus, the void within impenetrable. Twilight heard a soft, wet, slopping dissonance, a horrific inhuman sound that seemed to fill the chamber. There was an oozing, slithering grotesque quality to the sound, an abominable and repugnant vociferation that afflicted Twilight with an inner revulsion. His reaction was purely genetic, the deepest animalistic urge of fight or flight emerging to the forebrain of this supposedly civilized man. Twilight bared his yellowing teeth and an almost inhuman growl emerged from his chest, while his mind shrieked with terror at the unseen organism which appeared to be stirring within the shadow wrapped coffin.

A green beam of light emitted from the dark depths of the sarcophagus, striking Twilight in the chest and causing his body to seize up and freeze in place. The beam chased across his head, torso, moving with quick slicing movements across his body. There was a warmth to the light, yet Twilight was unable to move a muscle beyond his labored, slow breathing.

"Human," a gentle voice stated in his mind. "When we ruled this world, some of your people served us and we enhanced your capabilities. You have those same genetic qualities of our servant overseers. Your ancestors served my people and ruled your mammalian race. The slave behind you was of lesser stock. Such lesser creatures served until they were processed as food. You searched for us, you will serve us again. Correct?"

Twilight found himself able to answer, in his mind. The oddity of this form of speech should have shocked him, but he was suddenly filled with an odd, seemingly outside induced, calm at this time. "I will rule humanity?" he asked.

The unseen other seemed to chuckle, a bizarre sound that seemed rather inhuman in aspect. "Mammals. Your species is as rapacious as the lizards and the serpent races we created.

Yes, human. You will be a king or whatever title you wish. But to serve, you must awaken the tomb of the ancients. I am unable to seek the devices we require."

"If they exist still, I will look for them," Twilight replied, wondering what items this ancient being required.

"Your primitive technology could not damage the work of my people. You are not equipped for the search. Your body is weak, your mind weaker. I detect cancerous cells slowly awakening in your liver as well as a weakening of your kidney functions. Your use of opiates and fermented vegetative matter are destroying your weak, barely evolved physical form. You will be dead within two years. I will correct you. You will be capable of the feats you pretend to be able to perform for your slaves," the unseen master stated in Twilight's mind.

Twilight's eyes would have grown in shock if he was able to move. "I will be able to do magic?" he asked, a hopeful note in his mental reply.

The other replied with a grating sound in Twilight's brain that might have been a demoniac roar of laughter. "Magic? Your species still believes in such superstition? How amusing. No. What you call magic is mere energy manipulation. You will possess enough to rise above your kind. But your slave? Completely useless. Will you give it to me? I will provide one far more suitable and useful in your search."

Twilight felt a tiny trace of regret as he looked at his frozen patron. Lister's eyes were wild with terror, yet he appeared unable to move a muscle or even whimper in terror.

Twilight stated, "Take him." He didn't dislike Lister, but if the ancient rulers of the world needed him as food before they returned to Earth, so be it.

The other seemed to approve of Twilight's response. "Then let the work begin." A white beam of light covered

Tristan Twilight's body and he shrieked, a scream of pure agony as his body felt as if it was being torn apart. And then the source of the beams of power emerged from the murk and his screams of terror joined the wails of agony that emerged from his frozen lips.

⚡

TWO WEEKS LATER when Tristan Twilight and party emerged from the Gobi Desert, nobody seemed to remember the tall, pale English lord that was originally the co-leader of the group. He and a tall, robed figure left as soon as possible, their discussions held in hushed tones. Their destination was remarked upon by government officials and shippers who assisted in their plans for traveling away. They headed for a city in a land only heard of through travelers that passed through this region. A place of mystery in an odd country with strange customs.

⚡

NORFOLK, VIRGINIA: three months later.

THE NORFOLK DOCKS were surprisingly quiet as Lise Levi navigated through the narrow alleys nearby. Usually this area was teeming with life, sailors, longshoremen and hangers-on, all moving about, a multi-national sea of humanity. But tonight she was met with silence, few visible men and women, and the skittering of wharf rats searching for food. Lise liked the seafront area, the vaguely sinister sights and smells. The scent of the docks once again struck her like a fist. Rotting fish mixed freely with exotic spices, damp hemp with unidentified odors that caused her to blink and walk slightly faster without understanding why she reacted so strongly. The docks were a place unique to the world; none were alike and, even after visiting many, were still a source of interest to her.

Lise was a woman with short chestnut colored hair, high aristocratic cheekbones and hazel eyes that denoted a first-class intelligence. There was a wary quality about her; her bearing was confident, yet watchful. It was as if she was expecting attacks at any time and planned on paying the criminal back with a greater degree of violence. For this reason, and this alone, was she usually unmolested as she traversed these wharfs three times per week.

Finally, she arrived at her location, a small warehouse set apart from the others and surrounded with a large barbed wire fence. The gates opened as she approached, her stride never losing a step as she headed for the main building. There she spotted two men, both lounging against the wall of the large doors that led into the building. A sign over the doors read "MINOS SHIPPING COMPANY," though Lise never once heard anyone using such a title.

"Hey there, kid," Dirk Marat called out as Lise approached. He was a slight figure dressed in a white suit with a matching white fedora. Dirk was sharp featured, with light blond hair and dark eyebrows. There was a dangerous way about him, one that caused men and women to walk carefully when he was nearby. They unconsciously recognized this was a man of action who could handle himself in a scrap.

"Miss Levi," the other man stated with a slow nod. He was a giant of a man with bright red hair, enormous knobby fists, and a voice that sounded like the low rumble of thunder. Even the most daring brawlers on the docks stepped carefully around Red Argyle. His sheer muscular girth obtained him respect from even the nastiest quarters.

"Why are you two out here? And where's the chief? And why are the docks so quiet?" Lise shot back, taking in a breath and preparing to pepper the pair with more questions.

Red held up a large hand to stop the flow of words. "We can answer all the questions with one name. Captain Jason Seas."

Lise stopped in her tracks and cocked her head, thinking carefully for a moment. "Doctor Seas? The physician and historian?"

Dirk nodded quickly, an energetic and jerky motion, "He's buddies with the boss and they're working on something together inside. We prefer to stay out here when he's around."

"He's difficult to be around. When his ship is in town, the docks go real quiet. He can smell a crook a mile away," Red explained with a head shake. "He ain't fans of Dirk or me. In Dirk's case that makes sense."

"Shadap," Dirk replied, continuing the ever-running banter with his best friend. "What lit a fire under you, kid?"

Lise rolled her eyes at Dirk's continuing insistence of calling her "kid." It wasn't meant to make her feel weak or undermine her. Instead, it appeared he also called his younger sister, who lived in Des Moines or some such location, the same nickname. Red explained as much some months back, sensing Lise's growing annoyance at the name.

"The boss has me monitoring unusual activities around the world, ones that might be of interest to him. I found one that might mean something is about to occur," Lise explained, reaching into her handbag and pulling out a bundle of newspaper clippings. "Or better to say, something is occurring. I'm very concerned."

Before Dirk or Red could reach for the pages, the large warehouse door slid open. Two men emerged from the building, both impressive figures, even more so than Dirk or Red. The first was as large as Red, yet with even broader shoulders and smoothness of movement that even defied Dirk's calm actions. Dressed in a white peaked captain's hat and a pea jacket, Captain Seas had a leonine head of golden hair one associated with Vikings and an air of barely concealed fury.

The second was some inches shorter in height, but just as remarkable. This was Thunder Jim Wade, a legend in the world who few knew or ever met. At first glance, Wade did not appear to be such an extraordinary specimen of humanity. Tall, lean, and rangy, possessing a youthful energy that often made him look younger than his years. His hair was so black it almost appeared blue in the light and his dark eyes seemed deep and ancient, possessing both a soft depth as well as a harsh, dangerous coldness.

Seas' eyes scanned Dirk, Red, and Lise. It was a frank, appraising gaze, one that made Lise feel like an insect under a microscope. He glanced over at the impassive Wade and then back to Lise.

"Miss Levi," he acknowledged, his voice a deep bass. "Your paper on the lost origins of the Thule legend was well-presented, if sketchy on details. You have the same perspicacious mind as your late father. A sad loss."

He then turned his eyes on Dirk and Red, gave them a trace of a nod and stalked off. A roadster driven by a veiled woman in black pulled up by the gate and he climbed in, roaring off a moment later.

Dirk let out a long breath, suddenly relaxing, shaking his head. "Don't know why you like that guy, boss. He's a nasty one."

"Committed," Wade replied, his tone calm and without inflection. "The good Captain possesses strong views. He is committed to fighting for good. Also, his engineering skills regarding maritime crafts are unchallenged."

"You let him work on the *Thunderbug*?" Red asked, his deep voice rising. Despite his enormous size, Red possessed incredible deft hands and was a mechanical wizard.

The *Thunderbug* was the incredible craft of Thunder Jim Wade, a product of his unbelievable advanced sciences. The astonishing device was part boat, part submarine, part tank, and part plane, all capable of out-stripping the best in the world to date. How did Wade create such an advanced article of science? It came from his upbringing by a lost tribe in the heart of mysterious Africa. As a child he survived a plane wreck over a lost and hidden valley, one populated by a colony of people from the long-lost and mostly forgotten empire of Minos. The Minoans were a good people, a pacifistic tribe, whose science was far beyond modern man. Raised by the High Priest, Wade grew up to be a genius of science with skills and knowledge which he used to protect mankind from ancient evils. Under the guise of an adventurer, Wade and his aides were committed to fighting menaces mankind never knew existed.

Wade nodded once to Red, pulling out a small cigar and lighting it with a kitchen match. "I added a hover function to the *Thunderbug*. The transition between ocean and air was shaky at best. Captain Seas knew a method of improving performance."

"Huh," Red grunted, but clearly disliked the idea of anyone other than himself or Wade touching his beloved machine.

Lise, still stunned that the captain knew her and her father's work, stepped forward. This conversation on the *Thunderbug* could go on a long time and she did have a reason for leaving her office to come out here once again. Lifting the press clippings up, she stated, "That aside, I do need to speak to you, Mister Wade. I discovered information that might be of some concern."

Wade, Dirk, and Red all turned their full attention to Lise. The young woman possessed an incredible mind, capable of scrutinizing massive amounts of information and finding the one nugget of data that could lead to a greater issue. Born and raised in Germany by her father, an academic whose work on ancient mythology was well-known in those small circles, Lise fled with her parent to the United States for fear of arrest by the Nazis. Though young, she was as much as an expert as her late father and committed to using his knowledge to protect humanity. It was men like those that Wade fought that caused her father's untimely death, and Lise's skill made her an invaluable aide to Wade's crusade.

"Have you ever heard of Exham Priory?" Lise asked, lifting a copy of a small British paper.

Dirk and Red shook their heads, with Dirk asking, "Exham Priority? Is that a company?"

Red sighed loudly. "Priory, not priority, stupe. A priory is a religious house, where nuns and monks lives. There used to be one near the old mission back in New Mexico. Only ruins, but it used to spook us kids."

"Exham Priory," Wade broke in before Dirk could send back a quick rejoinder, "was the home of the de la Poer family. They had a checkered history. Full of tales of black magic and secret, unholy rites. At least five were executed as witches."

Lise nodded vigorously. "And one was killed by her

husband and mother-in-law. They confessed the reason for their murder and were absolved by the authorities and the church. The new Baron de la Poer's father revived the title but they've stayed away from the priory."

"I'm guessing something happened at that Exham Priority," Dirk said, knowing the malapropism would irritate Red. "Something spooky. Cause you seem a little rattled, kid."

Lise nodded again. "The building itself was destroyed. An American member of the family was restoring it for a time. Then he went insane and committed acts so vile my father wouldn't tell me what he did. That man died in an asylum. It was known there were caverns under Exham Priory, filled with huge rats."

Wade blew out a stream of smoke. "Your point?"

"A cavern was unearthed, a large hole dug into it releasing these rats upon the nearby woods and town. When the authorities discovered the source, they ventured into the depths. A small obsidian stone altar was found with ancient runes etched on the side. One word was translated: Tsathoggua."

Wade started, looking for a split second as if he was shocked by Lise Levi's revelation. Then his handsome face became carefully neutral. He tossed his cigar aside and said, "Get back to your homes and prepare for a long trip. Desert clothes as well as winter wear. Be back here in one hour."

"Something wrong, chief?" Red asked, surprised by their leader's strong, if momentary, reaction.

Wade nodded once. "More than you can possibly realize. If I'm right, this could mean the end of the world."

With that, Wade walked back to the hangar and out of sight. His three aides stared after him for a moment before running for the roadster parked near the gate. None had ever seen their leader so shaken by a piece of information. This alone was enough to tell them he wasn't exaggerating the terrible nature of what they were about to seek!

⚡

THE ODOR OF burnt rat filled the air, a harsh scent that permeated every corner of the tiny temple. The smell briefly disguised the overwhelming and overpowering fetor of putrescence that was as common as air in this underground realm. This was a microcosm of entropy, a world in which degeneration was all-encompassing and the denizens embraced the decay with open arms. For almost sixty years, this small circle of residents dwelt in the malodorous darkness, ignoring the outer world and embracing their slow transformation into something far less than human.

The oldest of the thirteen members reached out to the charred meat with a hairless gray-skinned extremity that was once a human hand. Now the fingers resembled the limbs of a hideous spider, each ending in long, hooked claws that gleamed dully in the spare light. The talons slowly sliced the cooked vermin into thirteen equal pieces, each of which he handed to the squatting creatures that were his followers.

These were once the leading members of the cult known as the Church of Starry Wisdom, Chicago chapter. Led by Professor Russell Graham, M.D., PhD Divinity, DPhil Ancient History, they were a rising sect in the growing city, a hub of the United States. Their mysteries intrigued many leading lights of Chicago, parvenus all, but many possessing a desire for the styling of European nobility. They were easy recruits for an Eastern old-money philosopher who humorously preached a Christian sect that allowed greater indulgences than the most Dionysian cults of ancient days.

The truth of the Church's true philosophy was known to a spare few, twelve other than Graham. Their sect worshiped an ancient being forgotten in time, known in whispers by many names. Called the Haunter of the Dark, the Three-Lobed Eye, the Dark One, and so many other names, this entity was their master, their only reason for being. Fanatics one and all, the Church of Starry Wisdom hid their repulsive deprivations behind a veneer of humor and extreme indulgences. For a time, they were a growing power in the city, advisers to the leaders of Chicago, experts at using the political corruption for their gain.

But then *He* came, out of the East, as knowledgeable as Russell Graham but a warrior determined to destroy the followers of the Outer Gods. The Church of the Starry Wisdom fell from power, their rites interrupted when their macabre machinations were about to come to pass. The backlash was horrendous, creating a conflagration that nearly consumed the entire city. Yet the leaders of the Church, the inner circle of thirteen, survived. Fleeing into the depths of the earth, they huddled in the Stygian depths and a slow metamorphosis commenced.

They were all now unrecognizable by eyes of modern man, the transformation tapping into ancient traces of a near human race that existed within the depths of all humanity's genetic legacy. Their skulls were now narrower, elongated and canine in appearance. Their eyes were larger, black in color and possessing no visible iris or pupil. The formerly proud, well-dressed group now clothed themselves in dusky rags, their twisted faces hidden beneath tattered hoods. And since the great blaze they sat, squatting in their moldering church, only rising to hunt for meat or to worship their dark deity.

Their small feast complete, Graham stood, waiting as his followers prostrated themselves before him in a circle. He then began to chant, his voice sounding more like the yips and barks of a large dog than a well-educated human. The others replied in the same guttural tongue, a rote formula repeated daily since coming to their dark sanctuary.

"Pathetic," Tristan Twilight stated, interrupting the Church of the Starry Wisdom's rites. He knew the words these base creatures were attempting to form, a lost language he learned fully since leaving the Gobi Desert.

"Intruder!" Graham snarled, pointing his clawed hands in Twilight's direction. The inner circle all rose to their feet, their hands as horrifically animalistic as their leaders, their faces and eyes even more inhuman.

"Meat!" Betty French hissed, a line of yellow drool forming at the ends of her black lips. Formerly a debutant and heiress of a family in the shipping business, she was unrecognizable, a perverted twisted relic of a once lovely woman.

Twilight stepped forward, his eyes pulsing red in the dim light. "Kneel, all of you," he whispered. His voice did not echo in the small chamber but seemed to carry to all the inner circle's ears.

The inner circle members, one by one, fell to their knees, their heads bowed in subservient submission. Finally, Graham dropped, unable to resist the overwhelming command of Twilight's single word.

"You were once the Church of the Starry Wisdom. Now you are my dogs, my hunting hounds. You will feed well if you serve me," Twilight intoned, disgusted by these creatures. But he had need for them; their twisted, terrible forms could prove useful in the coming days.

"Why do we need these things?" the Servitor asked, still covered in the robes obtained from the Gobi.

Twilight sighed in annoyance again, wishing this being was more subservient, less demanding. But the question was a good one this time. Waving a hand languidly towards the kneeling creatures, he explained, "These things last were in possession of one of the keys. When the key was removed from their possession, they were twisted by the power they no longer were able to control."

"That does not explain why you sought them in these catacombs," the Servitor replied acidly.

Twilight smiled slightly, "They are attuned to the key. Once we begin to search, they will lead us there with greater haste. Otherwise we could be searching for weeks. As I said, hounds."

The Servitor was silent for a moment and then nodded. "That has some logic. Where do we proceed?"

"Based on my research, I believe the key is hidden beneath a city of holiness, horror, and intrigue. A city called Rome," Twilight explained and waved the Servitor ahead. Snapping his fingers once, the former men and women of the Church of Starry Wisdom Chicago branch loped behind. Their new master promised them food!

⚡

ROME WAS A city in flux. An ancient capital filled with relics dating back to the days of the Etruscan Kings, there was a movement of modernity sweeping through the haunted ruins that dotted this land. Under the heavy hand of Il Duce, Benito Mussolini, an attempt to create a modern metropolis out of the ancient lands was in place.

With the subtlety of the Vandals and the Visigoths in ages past, the Blackshirts under their supreme leader attempted to push Rome towards the future.

But the city resisted, quietly and with the secret power that preserved her lands throughout the days when armed men sacked the city for personal gain. Rome outlasted many warlords and tribes long past, the Etruscans, Greeks, Romans under Marius, Sulla, Julius Caesar and many Emperors, Gauls, Ostrogoths, Holy Roman Empire, and French. All had their time to rampage through the elder municipality, all left lesser than when they arrived in the end. Certain cities possessed that power, a patient, primordial sentience which permeates the very land. And violators of these lands were slowly weakened, discovering that the luck that ruled so heartily in the favor for years was gone and never to be regained.

Which was why many denizens of Rome merely rolled their eyes at the demands of the ranting, theatrical little man who sat atop the political hierarchy at the time. Life would continue in the city, despite the demands of the weak men who sat at the fascist's side. The darkness, like the period before the many ancient sacks of Rome, was growing. Rome, the living entity, knew that an abysmal evil was coming soon and there was little anyone could do to resist the terrible tide. Few realized this hidden truth, but a select number, an unconnected society of those sensitive to such deeper truths, recognized the signs. Many of them were discounted as mad or foolish; such was the fate of all that sense the hideous fate that looms above men and lands throughout time. The gift of foresight into events is also a curse, for none would listen and react until the doom is clearly upon the victim. Thunder Jim Wade possessed a trace of this legacy, an unexpected gift from his ancient, unknown ancestors.

It was only in the years to come that Wade would learn of the true power that controlled and propped up Hitler, Mussolini, and their henchmen, the evil mind that nearly brought all the world to ruin. But in this day, when great powers were rising and threatening war, he would curse his lack of comprehension. The shadowy ruler, the great chess player of humanity he would later face, was still an unknown entity, a being only spoken in whispers to a spare few. His puppets in Germany, Italy, and elsewhere appeared to be the gangsters promoting their own brand of evil, and that was more than enough to focus upon at the time.

"Which catacombs are our destination?" Lise asked, trying to break the tense silence Wade cast upon their group. Their leader was never a chatty man, but he was answering them in clipped tones, each with an edge that brooked no response.

"There's more than one?" Dirk asked, sounding surprised. "They burying them three deep down there or something?"

"There's forty or so," Red answered and grinned at the looks of surprise on the faces of Lise and Dirk. "I looked it up in one of the boss's books before we left. The book said there's about forty and they were started by the popes to bury their dead from invaders."

"The book was wrong," Wade stated, turning the roadster into a busy Roman street. "The earliest tunnels were found by the Etruscans and the early Roman tribes. Other catacombs were built above them in tribute to the ancient artistry."

"Who built them?" Lise asked, once again amazed by Wade's incredible and detailed knowledge of pre-history.

"You don't want to know," Wade stated and suddenly pulled the roadster over by the side of the road, and everyone hopped out. He led them down an alleyway and walked into a tiny white brick chapel that was situated between the two buildings. The church was an ancient building, an early pre-Christian structure whose polytheistic images were systematically chiseled out by followers of latter day religions. The devastation of the early icons gave the diminutive house of prayer a skeletal countenance, a diminished quality. The fanatical assault upon the ancient religious spirits appeared to rob the church of all of its sacerdotal power, and the crucifix hanging above the minuscule stone altar gave the building a sad, ghostly atmosphere.

Wade walked to the altar, placed his hands on the edge and pushed. His cable like thews appeared to bunch and grow and a moment later the stone slid aside noiselessly. A small square passage was revealed with crude stone steps leading into a murky darkness.

"Boss," Red stated, his deep voice sounding concerned. "We would have helped you move the big stone. You ain't got to do it all alone."

It was Lise who shook her head, "I've read of such passages. The stones are weighted in a way so that only two hands can move it. More than two touching them would cause the altar to collapse and destroy the passageway. This was a method of protecting the catacombs by the builders."

Wade gave a short nod and intoned, "This passage leads to a part of the Catacombs of Saint Domitilla, the largest set of tunnels. From there we will take a hidden sub-tunnel into a set of caves deeper beneath the city. From there, we enter a very dangerous place. Do exactly as I order without question."

All three aides nodded, exchanging a look of concern. They were troubled by the clipped and dangerous way Wade was speaking, an edgy quality that never seemed to appear until Lise presented him with the information about the temple of Tsathoggua underneath the Exham Priory ruins. This quality was something they all sensed beneath the surface, a menacing aspect of the adventurer's personality that was held in careful control always.

Pulling out a clear round ball, Wade squeezed it once and a strong yellow light began to glow. Without a word he began to ascend the stairs, his step careful as he descended into the depths of the earth. Dirk, Lise, and Red each followed in that order, their steps even more careful than their leader. The steps were roughly cut and uneven, smaller than normal in height and spacing. This caused the enormous Red to step two and often three at a time, his stride being far too large to accommodate the tiny landings. The walls were roughly carved, chiseled out of stones through hard physical power without any form of artistry or planning. It seemed as if the very ground was torn open by a giant leaving behind a jagged rip leading into the bowels of the earth.

The air was surprisingly rich and full of dozens of different scents. Dust, rotting vegetables, spices, foods of different varieties and, surprisingly roses. It was as if the distant ancient resting places of the dead below their feet were also deeply connected to the city above their heads. All three aides exchanged a look, never having experienced such an odd connection between the surface and the world beneath their feet. It felt...wrong, an eldritch link that appeared to be an imperfection in the fabric of the universe.

Partway through the spiraling staircase, Wade indicated they should stop and move no further. His large, tanned hand suddenly began feeling along the beveled, jagged wall for a moment. He then pressed a rounded section of the rock, causing the stone to move inward imperceptibly. Several seconds later a slight scraping sound emerged from above their heads and the trace of light from above suddenly vanished. Somehow, obviously through some mechanism built into the structure, Wade was able to close the secret opening in the chapel above their heads.

"That is far more advanced than any structure I've read of in the past," Lise stated, breaking the tense silence.

Wade glanced over his shoulder, his dark eyes fixing on the young German academic. "The builders used techniques well beyond modern technology," he replied.

Dirk shook his head and snorted with annoyance, "There's some stuff you're holding back, boss. Care to clue us in?"

Wade fixed his steely gaze upon Dirk and frowned. "We don't have the time. If you trust me, then just understand that I hope all my suppositions are incorrect. If they're not, the whole world is in danger."

It was Red who spoke up fastest, though the others echoed his sentiment. "We trust you, boss."

Wade didn't reply or even give a hint he heard their affirmation. He merely turned back to the stairs and led their way farther into the depths. They reached the bottom of the staircase, their feet crunching slightly on the thin layer of dust on the stone floor. They were standing in a narrow corridor, unlit except by the small globe in Wade's fist. The ceiling and walls were pitted and coarse, their uneven surfaces adding deeper shadows to the ancient tombs. Four rectangular openings in the walls were visible down the hallway, each murky voids, impenetrable for the eye to pierce.

These were the ancient resting places of the dead, an open graveyard filled with miles of mummified remains, many little more than moldering piles of dust with the scraps of cloth of pieces of bones visible. This was a crypt without the benefits of a coffin, a massive mausoleum containing millions of the ancient departed. Even the sections lit by Wade's glowing globe appeared to be crushed beneath a powerful glowing layer of gloom. The Catacombs of Saint Domitilla were a disconsolate locale, an underground world crushed beneath the misery of human suffering and loss. Only Wade appeared unaffected as he strode down the hallway, his eyes scanning each of the graves with suspicious regard.

A few moments later, Wade stopped and looked above a low arch. The traces of carvings of a bearded man, his hands raised above the head of a kneeling woman. The indistinct quality of the art made it impossible to identify the man or who he was blessing. There was a subtle beauty to the nearly lost image, possibly a slight power based in the faith of the long-forgotten artist. Lise, Red, and Dirk stared at the etching, suddenly feeling slightly lighter in this domain of the dead.

Wade stepped slowly beneath the arch, his steps exact and measured. He stopped before a blank area of the wall and studied the rock for a moment. He then pushed two locations at the same time with his hands and a low click could be heard by all present.

"Whatever you do, do not move forward," Wade stated, raising one hand their way. "The very tread of your feet could set off the protective devices."

Dirk rolled his light-colored eyes with open exasperation. "Boss," he stated, sounding irritated, "this place is a boneyard. The only thing we have to fear is getting lost in this crazy maze."

Lise shook her head. "Ancient builders often added traps to protect their secrets. Many worked thousands of years later."

Red nodded, placing a large, calloused hand on Dirk's shoulders. "Think about that gear upstairs. I'd be hard pressed to find a way to do that now. If the chief says this place has traps, believe it. Okay?"

Dirk waved a hand to indicate he would yield to the request. "Still seems like a bunch of hooey to me. But I ain't moving."

Wade nodded and carefully moved his hands along the wall, finally stopping at a tiny outcropping. He pushed the rock slow, watching it recede inward several inches. Another loud clack could be heard, followed by soft scraping sounds from several locations. A slight vibration could be felt through the soles of their feet and then eerie stillness filled the tomb. The wall by the tomb gaped open, a space wide enough for the titanic figure of Red.

"Follow me," Wade stated and climbed into the rectangular tomb which lay next to the wall he manipulated.

"Um," Red stated, his face paling. "Climbing into a coffin...that's bad luck!" The giant man was notoriously superstitious, believing many old wives' tales and ancient legends he learned from his childhood in the Mississippi Delta. There, his family, dirt poor and working as sharecroppers, raised him to respect the many tales of the region and beyond. Luck and how the most elusive of objects could change your world were often the main points of the stories. The giant Red still respected many of these customs, preferring to err on the side of caution where bad juju was concerned.

Dirk rolled his eyes again and guffawed lightly, "That ain't a coffin, stupe! It's a fake one to hide the secret tunnel. The hoodoo won't come over and make you fall down an open manhole."

Lise laid a soft hand on Red's enormous arm and said, "The ancient designers of that passage wouldn't create a real tomb. That would be sacrilege. They'd have made it look real, so nobody could tell this was the passage."

Red frowned, but nodded, watching as Dirk climbed into the dark opening. Lise followed and vanished from view. Gulping audibly, Red slowly climbed inside and spotted an opening in the rough wall, one barely large enough for him to squirm through. The light from Wade's globe was distantly visible and a small comfort as he wiggled through the hidden trap door and was helped to stand by Dirk. The small hidden doorway closed with a low snap, cutting them off from the Catacombs of St. Domitilla.

They were now standing in a sloping declining cave, a smooth-walled corridor that led downward into a Stygian darkness. The air was clean and crisp, surprisingly fresh for the depth. The structure was unlike any cave any of the adventurers had ever experienced after their many travels. It was as if a giant drill bored through the rock, leaving behind an even surface that could never be created by natural elements. Little did they know-these stones were the same as the mineral shaping the tomb found by Twilight in the Gobi.

"Who built this...this hallway? The word is quite inadequate, but this was not made spontaneously. This is man-made!" Lise stated, staring around her in awe.

"Not man," Wade replied, "think far more ancient." He turned away, leading them deeper into the depths of the earth. The incline was gradual but seemed to spiral downward without any end in sight. Yet the air was almost too fresh, resembling a spring day after a short rain storm. While cool air and humidity were not unusual in underground structures, this atmosphere felt more alive than one would expect so deep beneath the surface. It was almost as if they were walking through a gentle meadow rather than an ancient, apparently designed cave made by hands other than mankind. Another oddity in this journey beneath the surface of the world.

The passage continued ever downward, the gradual slope causing them to feel as if time was no longer passing. It was as if they entered an endless spiral downward, an unchanging tunnel with no end in sight. The total lack of attributes to the tunnel added to the timeless unreality of their downward walk. Finally, Wade raised a dark-skinned hand and indicated they should stop.

"Boss," Dirk whispered as his keen senses provided him a trace scent only he could sense. "I smell blood. Not regular stuff. It's...it don't smell right."

Wade closed his eyes and very quickly entered a trancelike state. Slowly his senses began to recede, their perceptions vanishing from his mind and body. This was a skill he learned from the priests of the lost city of the Minoans. Minoans were far advanced in the secrets of the mind and body to the Western world. This skill, the ability to focus one's senses so completely they appeared more advanced and sharp than the human norm, served Wade on many occasions.

The blood which Dirk smelled was present, about fifty feet away and spread about over a wide demesne. There was a coppery human scent to the fluid, but this odor was only the smallest trace present. A putrescent malodor overlaid the spilled lifeblood, a tainted contamination with only a hint of humanity remaining. Forces beyond the imagination of man twisted the destroyed creature, removing its humanity and leaving behind a horrific monstrosity. The stench was overwhelming and Wade nearly wretched in disgust.

Opening his eyes and reactivating his other senses, Wade

frowned and nodded. "That thing was once a human. But it was transformed into something terrible. We've reached the first obstacle. The trap is said to be lethal and bring about a slow, painful end."

"Who lived here? You said the Etruscans were not the first," Lise retorted, crossing her arms across her chest. "All science to date refers to them as the eldest inhabitants of this region."

"The Etruscans were approximately the twentieth tribe who lived in this region, if I remember correctly. The Corinthians, Koth, and Ophir all occupied this territory, and even they were late-comers. No, the beings who made these tunnels were foul and frightening. They subjugated all life to slavery and were finally destroyed when humanity and other races rose up in rebellion," Wade instructed. "Now, follow me. We're close to the trap."

They strode slowly around the next bend and stood before an immense chamber. The walls were of the same unadorned, smooth stone and the vaulted ceiling was at least forty feet above their heads. A huge dark stain festooned the center of the room, the globe of light in Wade's hand causing the surface to glisten lightly in the spare illumination.

"How's this trap work, Chief?" Dirk asked, covering his nose and backing away from the entrance. He could clearly see the blood on the floor, the exact shape of the stain and smell the noxious aroma of the fluids. Dirk possessed senses that even rivaled Wade. Unlike the great adventurer, Dirk was occasionally overwhelmed by the sheer volume of sensations that surrounded all beings on the Earth. It was only by concentrating strongly, focusing on one detail that Dirk was able to ignore the more pernicious smells and sights that surround all life on Earth.

Wade shook his head. "No idea. I've never read anything other than the existence of dangers in these tombs and others like it. But I do know there's always a means of disarming the murderous device."

"You mean like that lever up over our heads?" Red asked, pointing a sausage-sized finger straight up towards the room's roof.

There it was, a metal shaft protruding from the wall well above their heads. It was only the glowing globe in Wade's hand that allowed them to see the location of the object. The lever itself was made of black metal and would have been impossible to see without a lot of luck.

"Toss up a line and pull," Dirk said and pulled out a silken line that was immensely strong. A gift from a crime fighter they met years before when he was killing a gang of criminals that were threatening to murder thousands. The crime fighter was dangerously insane, but on the right side at least. And this thread was as thin as a spider's web but nearly as hardy as metal wire.

Red shook his huge head quickly. "No! Bad idea! Are you out of your tiny brain?"

Dirk frowned and gave Red the gimlet eye. "What are you yammering about, lummox?"

Red waved a massive arm up towards the lever, "Your idea is about as goofy as those toys you like to toss around. What if there's a lock attached and the handle breaks? Or you need to push it up? Or to the side? You'll bust the only way we have to get through in one piece!"

"Okay, okay, keep your shirt on," Dirk replied, putting the rope away. He didn't question his giant friend's knowledge of machinery, even ones created by ancient, advanced beings. "It was just an idea."

"We can do it the hard way," Wade stated, ending the interplay between his aides. He didn't mind their playful bickering, but there were limits. "Red, make a table."

Red didn't reply, he merely dropped down on his hands and knees and braced himself against the ground. Wade stepped onto his back, checked his footing, and nodded at Dirk. Dirk scrambled onto Red's back and, without hesitation, climbed onto Wade's shoulders. A moment later Wade was lifting him up, balancing the lean Dirk with the strength of his arms. This was an amazing feat of acrobatics, one Wade and his men practiced in case they were trapped, for a third time, in a deep pit.

"I'm about four feet short!" Dirk called down. "Red will have to stand up so I can reach."

"Won't work. Balance will be precarious at best," Wade replied, frowning and thinking of an alternative.

"Oh, for heaven's sake!" Lise Levi snapped and rolled her eyes. A few seconds later she stepped onto Red's huge back and stepped before Wade. "Bend your knees and brace yourself."

Wade smiled slightly and complied, bending his knees and supporting Lise's weight as she climbed up onto his shoulders. His arms did not shake, but the mighty thews along his shoulders and back bunched, tightened, and loosened like the movement of a massive leopard stalking its prey.

Dirk grinned as Lise scaled his back and sat down on his shoulders. "Good move, kid. Can you reach it?"

"Yes," Lise replied. She paused and studied the device before calling down, "The lever moves upwards. The handle is covered in blood."

"Don't let the blood touch your skin. If any gets into

your bloodstream, you could be infected. Use your gloves," Wade cautioned. He couldn't see what Lise was doing, but a moment later heard the grinding of gears and a loud thud fill the chamber as the trap was disarmed. A pair of gloves were tossed into the room from above, striking the stone floor with soft slaps.

Wade lowered Dirk and Lise to the ground gently and hopped off Red's back. Red stood up with a grunt, stretching his body and causing his back to pop several times. The sound was like soft gunshots, but the massive man appeared otherwise unaffected by bearing the weight of two men and one woman.

Leading them around the drying bloodstain in the room, Wade stopped as they were about to enter another tunnel which spiraled sharply downward. Not having time to once again focus his senses, he turned to Dirk and nodded towards the featureless cave. Wade didn't need to explain what he required, his aides were all aware of his thoughts through his smallest gestures.

Dirk stepped forward sniffed once and nodded. "Yeah, they went down that way. Not too long ago."

"How do you know?" Lisa asked, genuinely curious.

Dirk shrugged. "Some of them stepped in the blood. They carried that stink down with them. It's strong. Worse than a slaughterhouse and a fertilizer plant pushed together. I mean like Red's BO after he's been working on the *Thunderbug*."

"Or Dirk's aftershave. What's it called, Eau du Toiletbowl?" Red shot back.

Wade raised a hand to stop the flow of invective that was about to start. "They're following the tunnels. This will allow us a chance to get to the tomb ahead of this group."

"How will we manage to pass them in a small channel

through the rocks? We had to walk single file," Lise asked. Her leader's mysterious behavior was starting to annoy her. But she refrained from demanding answers, knowing Wade was unlikely to do so anytime soon.

Wade walked into the cave, stepping slowly. He stopped and, with a gentle touch, began feeling along the left side wall. Suddenly he pushed two locations and stepped closer to the group, watching. The wall slowly ebbed backwards, the movement fluid, almost liquid as the stone appear to vanish. A round opening was left behind and within was a stygian murk so substantial it appeared to be a solid wall.

"Maintenance shaft. This will get us to the bottom far faster. Though I cannot determine the traps and details, all of these structures have these shafts," Wade explained and pulled out his silken line. All three aides did the same and watched as Wade wrapped a sticky blue paste around the end of the cords, binding them together. This was another of his incredible inventions, a powerful adhesive that dried within seconds.

With all their ropes bound together, Thunder Jim added a little more to the end and slapped it to the wall. He then tested it twice and stepped into the void, vanishing from view. Dirk, Lise, and Red each followed, the light of Wade's globe the only illumination in the dark. The shaft was a mass of shadows, with an impression of vastness that could not be realized by the climbers. It felt as if they were climbing into a bottomless chasm, a tunnel whose depths ended at the legendary center of the earth.

There were wide outcroppings that allowed stops for breaks, since the trek by rope was arduous to all save Wade. His silent yet resolute presence caused his three aides a small uplift of spirit. The descent was grueling and punishing, taxing upon their muscles as they moved deeper through the maintenance shaft of the ancient tomb.

"Boss," Red said as they hit the bottom and Wade gave them each time to recover. "That took forever and week. How will we beat them down here?"

"The spiral they are taking is meant to take a great length of time to complete. According to legend, there are at least five traps they will have to confront. Either way, we're in the lead." Wade explained and handed each of his team a small capsule to swallow. The pills were an herbal mixture that revitalized the body. Each of the herbs included were incredible rare and difficult to cultivate, which was why he was sparing with providing them even to his closest friends.

Seeing his aides were stronger again, Wade led them down a small cave which opened into a boxlike room made of black bricks. A large passageway lay at the far end of the room, which spiraled up and out of sight. Moving to the right side of the room, Wade counted bricks for a few seconds and reached for the stone with both hands. Spreading his fingers in an odd pattern, Wade held his breath and steadily increased the pressure in an equally strange order.

For a moment, nothing happened. Then a panel slid aside in the wall, revealing a gray metal shelf covered in multifaceted jewels. The stones appeared to be softly glowing, twinkling like tiny stars and caused the room to glow with a soft, comforting ambiance.

Exhaling, Wade waved his aides to silence strode over to the shelf and studied the gems without a sound. His eyes scanned the jewels and his lips moved silently as he remembered the lore he learned from his people. Wade then visibly relaxed and pressed four of the stones in quick succession. Several feet from where he was standing, the floor opened, and a large oblong cylinder slid into view. It was about seven feet high and made of the same metal as the shelf containing the jewels. There was a chill about the rounded box, a harsh cold that caused Wade's three aides to step back without thought.

"What in the holy heck is that? Santa's coffin?" Dirk asked, fingering one of his namesake knives.

"It ain't right, whatever it is. That's like the cold you feel in a graveyard. Bad luck," Red added, pulling his flame gun out and holding the weapon at his side.

Lise studied the object, surprised at her frightened reaction to it. She normally dealt with all situations as a scientist, an explorer into mankind's past. Rarely did she possess an opinion on ancient objects. They were simply relics of the past, something to be studied. But this metal tube, unadorned by etchings or carvings, this item repulsed her. "I agree with Red. I don't like it. What is it?"

"It was a coffin for the ancients," Tristan Twilight stated from the doorway. He smiled as the four adventurers started with surprise. Dressed in a clean, pressed white suit, white shirt and tails, he presented a ghostly, rather than saintly, image. His sneering smirk revealed to anyone his complete lack of virtuous spirit.

"How did you know that?" Wade whispered, surprised this man had knowledge of such hidden and lost data.

"I'd like to know that too, Tristan Twilight!" Lise Levi snapped, her face blazing with fury. "This man is nothing a cheap carnival showman, a poseur! My father drove him out of Germany before the Nazis took over, revealing his secret knowledge was nothing more than illiterate scraps of half-understood gibberish!"

Twilight's smile flickered slightly, and his eyes narrowed,

giving his now thinner face a porcine appearance. "You're the daughter of that decrepit senile bastard, Isaac Levi? Is he alive? I hope so. He cost me a chance at a Prussian title and a fair living."

Lise shook her head. "No. Why would you care?"

"I wanted the chance to kill him slowly and painfully. I'd draw it out for months, watching him suffer. I'll settle for you, his daughter. You can start by kneeling to me. Kneel!" Twilight's voice was a sibilant, serpentine hiss. This was an inhuman sound, as if a creature from the depths of madness were suddenly alive and demanding worship.

Lise wanted to tell Twilight to drop dead or some other, far worse, oath. But she found herself unable to speak. Instead, slowly, her knees began to bend. She fought, her mind screaming as her legs slowly lowered her towards the stone floor of the cave.

Wade pulled Lise to her feet, staring with narrowed eyes at Twilight. "Enough! You will not attack my people!"

Twilight shook his head slowly, "Wrong to both questions. I will reduce your little band of soldiers-of-fortune to sniveling slaves begging for my mercy. Starting with the legendary Thunder Jim Wade. Drop to your knees and beg to serve me. Now!"

Wade felt the psychic force strike him like an icepick in his brain. The pain was immediate and harsh, but he resolutely held his ground. Only a twitch around his eyes betrayed the agony he was experiencing at the hands of Twilight.

"Nuts to that!" Wade snarled, "Dirk, kill him!"

Dirk, having palmed a knife earlier, flashed his hand forward towards Twilight. The blade flew directly for the English magus's exposed jugular vein, a true kill shot. Like his namesake, Dirk was a master of the knives, fighting or throwing he lived for the dangerous polished steel. He rarely ever missed.

The knife flew true, a silver streak of light aimed perfectly for Twilight's throat. A hand interposed between the magus and the blade sank deep into the limb. The hand did not belong to Twilight; it was long, pale and came from behind the Englishman. From the shadows behind him came the source, a tall figure covered in a gray, all-concealing robe. The Servitor stepped into view, as did the three surviving members of the cabal Tristan Twilight took over in Chicago. The cabal members crouched at their feet, gray-skinned and canine in aspect, both frightening and pathetic to the naked eye.

"What in the world are those things?" Dirk cried, staring at the former occultists whose inhuman eyes seemed to gaze at them with unconcealed rapacious hunger.

Surprisingly, it was Red who answered. "Ghouls, corpse eaters. We drove them off the local pauper's graveyard when I was growing up. They...they ain't right..."

Before anyone else could react, the Servitor pulled the knife out and tossed it to the ground. The blood on the blade was silvery and seemed to twinkle in the sparse light. Before their eyes, the upraised hand began to heal, sealing up in less than five seconds.

"They stand in our way. We must destroy them and complete our tasks," the Servitor whispered. The being was as tall as Red, but far slimmer despite the covering robes. The voice was flat, almost mechanical and inhuman sounding, the pronunciation of each word a shade too correct and precise.

Twilight sighed and nodded his head once. "Try and save the female. We can use her as a slave and a bit of fun."

The Servitor pointed at Wade and his group and

whispered again. "Feed. Feast on them, my pets."

With a bestial cry, one which echoed in the stone cavern, the ghouls bounded forward. Lise was the first to act, pointing her flame gun at the lead monster and firing a stream of liquefied heat. The creature was struck in the chest and squealed in agony. The ghoul's flesh ignited and the horrific creature fled back up the tunnel, wailing in torment. Wade and Dirk fired their flame guns a heartbeat later, hitting the monsters as expertly as Lise, sending them into wailing retreat after their brethren.

At the same moment, Red bounded forward, determined to pull down Twilight's protector. His huge hands sought to grab the Servitor's wrists and force the robed figure to the ground. But the Servitor, in a move as lightning quick as Wade, pulled both arms just out of reach. Red's gargantuan fingers snagged the end of the Servitor's robes, causing them to tear with an audible rip. He gasped in shock with what was revealed, his eyes widening in shock.

The being beneath the robes wasn't human, not by any stretch of the imagination. Though human shaped, the being appeared to be a gelatinous ooze. The creature appeared both solid and liquid, the torso moving, undulating, hardening and then mucilaginous with sinewy rope like tendons visible. Two oversized red orbs sat atop the head-shaped object on the monstrosity's apex, unblinking and moving independently from each other. A gaping maw was visible and rows of sharp ivory, triangular fangs sparkled in a lipless cavity.

"A Servitor!" Wade exclaimed, shaking his head in shock. "Your kind was hunted down and destroyed thousands of years ago!"

"You recognize us?" the Servitor asked. The voice that emerged from the creature possessed a sonorous sound, heavy and thick. The syllables sounded heavier normal, inhuman in timbre and sounding as if they were created by something other than lungs.

Twilight looked at the Servitor in surprise, "You never said your kind was killed off by humanity."

"You never asked," the Servitor replied, its attention entirely on Wade. "Your kind hunted my people to near extinction. Your death shall be small recompense. But it will suffice for the moment."

"Lise, Dirk, Red!" Wade called, "Point your guns at Twilight and the Servitor!"

All three of his aides immediately complied, pointing their flame weapons at the jewel-covered console near the rear of the chamber. These guns were designed and built by Wade for reasons known only to himself. The weapons were only slightly effective, but the adventurer insisted on their use over modern firearms.

"All three of you," Twilight intoned, his face still sneering, "point your weapons at Thunder Jim Wade. Fire on my command."

Slowly, fighting all the way, Lise, Dirk and Red each turned their bodies towards their leader. Sweat broke out on all three aide's brows, but this was the only hint they were attempting to fight Twilight's psychic control. Wade was standing near the console, the barrel of his gun mere inches from the metal shelf.

"Standoff," Wade said, looking at Twilight. "You get them to shoot me, the controls to the coffin go boom."

"The console can be repaired. You'll be dead and we'll still get what we came for today. There is no loss to me in any scenario, sir," Twilight replied, barely suppressing a giggle.

Wade looked at the Servitor. The creature was standing

frozen in place, horrid red eyes both fixed on the human adventurer. "Tell him."

"If the controls are destroyed, there is no means of repair. The creators are the only who comprehend the creation of their science," the Servitor stated, still staring at Wade. "You, human. You know too much of the ways of the ancient masters. How is this possible?"

"Wouldn't you like to know?" Wade said. "Release my people now, Twilight!"

Twilight considered the situation for a moment and then shook his head. "No. I will not yield my advantage to you. The three of you, place your guns against your heads."

Without pause, Lise, Dirk and Red each lifted their flame guns and placed it against their temples. Wade knew there was no way he could prevent the death of his aides unless he acted instantly. Slumping his shoulders in defeat, Wade dropped his flame gun to the ground. He was rewarded by Twilight's grin of triumph.

"Kick the gun over here, old boy. No Bulldog Drummond tricks, if you please," Twilight stated, chuckling.

That was Wade's opening. He kicked the flame gun straight up into Twilight's face, causing the magus to howl in surprise and pain. The spell holding Lise, Dirk, and Red was snapped and their weapon-filled hands dropped to their sides.

"Run!" Wade ordered and was rewarded by the lightning fast reactions of his aides. All three ran for the tunnel they used to get to the vault and were out of sight just as Twilight got himself under control. The Servitor still wasn't moving and watched Wade with the same horrific red eyes. The slits where a nose was located twitched, adding to the horrific appearance. Unarmed, Wade ran after his aides, dropping a metal tube behind him as he fled.

Twilight moved to follow, but was restrained by the hand of the Servitor.

"Do not follow. He has left behind a trap. It smells like an alchemical adhesive. You would be trapped for a day or more. It would take me several hours to free myself," the Servitor explained, pointing to the tunnel.

"Why didn't you mention that earlier? You were threatening the man mere seconds ago," Twilight snarled.

The Servitor's dreadful, loathsome orbs swiveled to Twilight. Though Twilight had spent much time in the company of this chimerical being, he was never comfortable when it focused upon him. "A glue would not assist the human. You were able to control his slaves. This rendered his assault a waste of time. But if we are both trapped, and he is free, our mission will fail. We must not fail the masters."

Twilight bit back a sarcastic reply, realizing this abhorrent being was correct. Returning the ancient masters of the earth to power was far more important than battling a nosy adventurer and his idiotic followers. Nodding, he walked over to the console and depressed a series of the glowing stones in a specific order. The large metal tube slid open, revealing a small black stone. Lifting it, Twilight marveled at the non-Euclidean angles that faceted this ancient artifact. He'd read of this object over the years, remembering it was owned by at least one ancient Egyptian Pharaoh and, according to legends, the creatures that ruled ancient Atlantis.

"The Shining Trapezohedron," he whispered, studying the face of the stone and smiling. "Only one more piece to go."

"The humans are well-informed. They may attempt to seize the third key," the Servitor said, a warning tone in its dehumanized voice.

"I'm counting on them to perform that act exactly. They shall do as we require, and we will deliver the final piece of the key as well as a sacrifice to the masters," Twilight stated, not taking his eyes away from the Shining Trapezohedron.

The Servitor was silent for several minutes. "That appears needlessly complicated. Why not merely take the third key from the mammals and kill them at that time?"

"Wade and his female injured me. The first physically, the latter through her decrepit fool of a parent. I will have my revenge upon them. It will be glorious!" Twilight replied, his voice growing in volume and pitch as he explained his plans.

"Vanity," the Servitor said, sounding disapproving despite the unearthly sounds of its speech. "An illogical attitude among your species. It appears to be a genetic anomaly that should be fixed when the masters return."

"Nonetheless," Twilight replied, handing the Shining Trapezohedron to the Servitor, "we will replace your robes and find another plane. We have some distance to cover. Follow me and I will explain."

⚡

AFTER A SHORT climb, Wade led his aides to an outcropping which possessed a secret entrance to the circular tunnel. The others followed him numbly, running with all their strength, ignoring their exhaustion as they finally reached the surface. Jumping into the roadster, they didn't stop until they were back at the airport. Climbing into the *Thunderbug*, they were off in the air in mere moments.

"Boss," Dirk asked, swiveling in the co-pilot's seat. "What in the holy heck happened down there? That Twilight mug had us doing whatever he said. I couldn't stop doing what he said!"

"Me too," Red agreed. He sat slumped in his seat, his huge body looking shrunken and worried.

Lise nodded but didn't speak. She looked enraged and frightened, barely in control of herself and was fighting for some measure of calm.

Thunder Jim Wade was silent for a long time, staring ahead as he controlled the incredible craft known as the *Thunderbug*. "Tristan Twilight was remade. Ancient terrible sciences by creatures from beyond the stars. They were believed destroyed, gone forever. But it looks like they're back."

"How," Lise asked through clenched teeth, "did a peddler of falsehoods like Tristan Twilight obtain such massive power? And why were you immune?"

"The first, I have no answer. As to my immunity. I was trained to control my mind and body by the priests of the Minotaur. His form of psychic attack is the first we are taught to resist," Wade explained.

"Yeah?" Dirk asked, as always surprised by the details of his leader's early life. He and Red had both travelled to the lost colony of the Minoans, but the details of that unusual civilization were still mysteries. "How can I learn it?"

"It would take several years, and you might not succeed. Also, don't fight the Servitor," Wade replied and glanced at his aides. "A Servitor is not easy to kill. Use your flame guns and run for your life. It will take it several minutes to rebuild itself."

"That thing can recreate itself when it's on fire? Then how do you kill it?" Red asked, looking nervous.

"I don't know," Wade admitted, "That information was

lost in time. All that I know is they can change their forms, be hard or liquid."

"Delightful," Lise grumped and crossed her arms across her chest. "Where are we going now?"

Wade adjusted his instruments slightly and said, "Palestine. Specifically, Jerusalem. The final piece of the puzzle was hidden there by the Knights Templar. Twilight has the Trapezohedron now and, I believe, the statue of dread Tsathoggua from the Exham Priory. Sit back, we'll be there in three hours, depending on the tailwinds."

Dirk, Lise, and Red exchanged a look. They all knew that, despite his explanation, there was a great deal Wade was holding back. The problem for them was not that their leader didn't trust them; no that wasn't an issue. It appeared he was more concerned that the full details would terrify them even more than they were now. And that, in and of itself, was more terrifying than Twilight's ability to control their minds. It was a subdued group that flew through the night.

⚡

JERUSALEM WAS UNQUESTIONABLY one of the most unique cities on Earth. One of the oldest metropolises in the world, this location had been the site of more battles than most realized. Jerusalem, historically, was destroyed at least twice, attacked dozens of times and captured by many ancient and modern empires. As the center of three major religions—Judaism, Christianity and Islam—the city possesses many locations of historic and spiritual significance. But Jerusalem was a land under occupation of the British where the various religions were in constant conflict. Jews battled Muslims, both sides battled the British. The war was on a smaller scale, violence with periods of peace, terrorism by all three sides followed by suspenseful anticipation.

Entering Jerusalem was often compared to taking a trip through time. Locations in the city varied wildly and often in ways that confused newcomers. Sections of the municipality dated back to the time of the Roman occupation. And there were areas that could be the outskirts of any major metropolis in the world. The sheer incongruity of the city created an environment few could decipher. Holiness and modernity side-by-side in an atmosphere of tense anticipation for the next outbreak of violence between the various factions.

Wade was surprisingly comfortable in this environment. The aberrative atmosphere reminded him of the shock he felt leaving the ancient, yet scientifically advanced lost city of the Minoans. Were it not for the many terrible secrets that lay hidden beneath the antediluvian stones, Wade would spend more time in this city. But his knowledge of the lost secrets of the world made him unable to settle in any location other than his private, secret island in the Pacific. There he could relax his mind, safe with the knowledge that he was in one the few places where little to nothing happened in the past. Jerusalem was a land of mysteries few comprehended in this day and age. Once the ancient land of Shem, the occupiers of this land were the subjects of an empire of horror and cruelty. The remnants of the long-destroyed and forgotten regime of demon worshipers still lay under the sands of this country as well as neighboring countries.

The thought of spending time in a place where such horrors might rise left Wade in a state of constant tense anticipation. And he, thanks to his extensive training under the Priests of the Minotaur, knew that attempting to live in such a manner would bring about his early demise. Therefore he monitored the land through agents and clipping services, but otherwise kept his visits short.

Landing the *Thunderbug* in a small airport, Wade made several adjustments to the miraculous device. Unfortunately, it would not serve any use in this city. The streets, many designed by the ancient Romans and earlier conquerors, were far too small for the *Thunderbug*.

"You three will wait with the *Thunderbug*. Only one person can get into where the final element is hidden. If more than one attempt to enter, great disaster will follow. If I'm not back in twelve hours, try and locate Captain Seas. His knowledge is imperfect, but he can help you with the future calamities that will follow," Wade explained, pocketing an extra flame gun and a heavy robe.

"You're not leaving us behind, Chief," Red stated, his deep voice sounding even rougher than usual. "You know we can help."

"I'm with Red," Dirk said, shaking his head. "We're a team, ain't we?"

Lise studied Wade for a moment and asked, "You have a secondary reason for not wishing us to follow you? Correct?"

Wade nodded once. "The place I am going is one of the most holy sites in the world. Three religions venerate the location. Few know this was chosen by King Solomon as a fortress as well as a temple."

"Explain," Lise demanded. "I assume you are referring to the Well of Souls."

"The well of what?" Dirk asked, "I'm not sure I heard that right."

It was Lise who answered, her academic training taking over, "The Well of Souls is a cavern beneath the Dome of the Rock. The Dome of the Rock is a shrine on Temple Mount in Jerusalem where the first and second temples existed. The dome, which is made of gold, houses the boulder in which Abraham is said to have sacrificed Isaac at God's command. This same boulder is where Mohammad ascended to heaven. The Well is a cave beneath the Dome. Sir Francis Burton explored it while visiting the city. It's said the Templars also used it for their rites. Nobody is allowed in anymore. There has never been any scholarship that holds the true use of the chamber."

"Correct," Wade replied, nodding a second time. Lise was an exceptional scholar, a true expert who had the potential to change the way mankind viewed the more unique side of history. If she hadn't chosen to work with his team, she'd no doubt be employed by one of the better universities, writing books. Lise rejected the notion, having chosen to join his team and fight the ancient evils that Wade was pledged to destroy. Making a choice, he decided to share what few in the world knew these days. "This information was never written down. Not even in hints."

"Why? Dirk asked, not wanting to be left out of the high-end discussion that was happening before his eyes.

It was, once again, Red who answered. "What's the best way to keep a secret? Don't speak or write it down. There's a lot of that in the world. The bad stuff out there loses power when it's hidden away."

"Correct," Wade repeated and gave his huge aide a rare smile. "To release the information would cause some to attempt to explore the very evil they were fighting. Under the name Astarte, this being, this Outer God, spread its filth. The rituals pretended to be fertility based. But in truth they were designed to bring about a race of monsters in the world. Ones who would clear the earth of all life. Then the Outer

Gods and their servants would return and repopulate the planet in their twisted name."

"Oh my," Lise said, her voice barely a whisper, "The Goat..."

Red visibly started, his massive fists bunching, the knuckles popping like pistol shots. "The Dark Mother. The Nightmare Woman."

"What in the heck are you talking about?" Dirk demanded. He knew his buddy Red was deep into weird, spooky stuff like juju and all that nonsense. This time his craziness seemed to spread to the boss and Lise. Dirk himself didn't believe in mumbo-jumbo, having been raised in a house where getting your next meal and not getting beat for making noise was more important than anything else.

"An ancient being that pretended to be a human god. The creature brought about fertility to the land and people, but the price was to infect them with inhumanity. When its true nature was discovered, mankind fought to quash it's power."

"During the Crusades, Saladin and King Richard fought together to put one of these cults to the sword. They respected each other from that day on." Lise added.

Red looked Dirk in the eyes, his fright evident. "My daddy and my granddaddy once told me about one of the things that came out of their practices. It had no head, three arms and one leg. It killed old man Jenkins and his wife before Mama Marie, the old wise lady sent it away screaming with a charm. I saw it once, at a distance on Pythian Hill, near the conjuring circles. It was screaming a name that caused my ears to bleed. That's why we moved to New Mexico, to get away from the bad stuff in the Delta."

Dirk wanted to scoff but, having served with Wade for so long, he knew better. There was more to the world than even he knew. And he'd seen stuff that would send writers, like the ones in that magazine *Weird Tales*, run screaming into the night. Which was why he just nodded and waited for the boss to conclude the lecture.

Seeing Dirk's acceptance, Wade concluded, "The creature's name is Shub-Niggurath. Her followers are known to cry during their dark sacraments, 'Iä! Shub-Niggurath! Iä! Shub-Niggurath! The Black Goat of the Woods with a Thousand Young.' And the children this Outer God produces are pure horror. You saw one before. A Servitor is one of the Black Goat's progeny."

"That don't tell me why only you can go into this Well place, boss. Let's bring it down to brass tacks. What's the problem?" Dirk asked, raising one dark eyebrow. "You three are so scared of this boogey-woman, you ain't thinking clearly."

"To enter the caverns beneath the Well of Souls is dangerous. Ancient monsters still reside down there, held back by powers I can't begin to comprehend. Even a second person is too great a risk. Also, if I fail, you three will need to try and find Tristan Twilight. Uniting the keys would bring about an apocalypse that even biblical scholars couldn't foresee. Please, all of you. Do as I say," Wade said, offering a rare plea to his three aides. His naked terror about the results of Twilight's mad plans was, if possible, more frightening than his dark predictions of the future.

Without a word of demure, Lise, Dirk, and Red each nodded their acceptance of their leader's orders. They seemed at a loss for words and were unable to speak until well after Wade left the *Thunderbug* and was out of sight.

"Start the timer, kid," Dirk said, his voice a little husky. "Red, let's get this buggy out of sight. That Twilight character may be behind us, but I don't want him and his whatchamacallit buddy to sneak up on us. No way, no how!"

✦

THE DOME OF the Rock, better known as Qubbat al-Sakhrah, was one of those sites in the world that demonstrated holiness in all its beauty. Atop the hill known as Temple Mount, this structure was not huge, but was a shining beacon possessing a power few could fail to feel. The outer walls were enclosed by Byzantine styled mosaics, each of which possessed an elder splendor reminiscent of the first churches built by that long-lost empire. The octagonal sides, while replete with the artistry of the millennium gone builders, were never gaudy or gauche. There was a majesty to these walls few structures ever managed to achieve, no matter their age. But the dome itself was the most striking feature, a golden vault that served as a beacon for Temple Mount for all who entered Jerusalem. The golden edifice glimmered in the harsh desert sun, a resplendent vault that caused even the most jaded to stare at the grandeur of this shrine.

The interior of the Dome was dark and sedate despite being covered with the same magnificent craftsmanship. Perhaps it was the low light, or the feeling of serenity one received within, but there was a holiness to the sanctuary that demanded respect from all.

The reliquary itself was a large boulder in the center of the shrine, surrounded by places for those who wished to kneel in contemplation or prayer. Biblical scholars held that this was the site where Abraham bound Isaac for sacrifice at the command of the Lord. The Christians held that this stone is where Jesus stood and preached his words of love and peace to his followers. The prophet Muhammad, according the scholars of the Koran, mounted this boulder before ascending to heaven at the side of the archangel Gabriel.

The Dome itself was the vision that overwhelmed all who enter the sanctum. Spiraling above the golden arch, enveloped by scrollwork and mosaics that possess such fine detail, they were impossible to discern in one viewing. The imagery appeared almost alive, the beauty and craftsmanship reaching a level of skill nearly impossible for mankind.

There were locations in the world where religion and artistry met, and the result was a structure possessing a majesty that outstripped the petty concerns of mankind. The Dome of the Rock, Michelangelo's ceiling at the Sistine Chapel, the Wailing Wall of Temple Mount, and the four carvings of Buddha of Gal Viharaya in Ceylon were examples of such amazing religious locales. To enter the presence of these places of worship caused many to feel closer to their respective religious figure. This was one of the heights of the craft of an artist, where their work achieved heights that transported the pilgrim or onlooker to a connection with the icon that was central to the work.

Thunder Jim Wade was raised in such a location; the temple of the Minotaur in the lost city of the Minoans was just such a place. And since returning to civilization, he took the time to visit each of the important religious sights, viewing them with the reverence and respect they deserved. The Dome of the Rock, like the others, was a place he felt at peace. He would have like to have spent time meditating in the serene environment, but sadly this was not to be this time.

Wade pulled the hood of his robes a little further over his head and moved to the cave beneath the rock better known as the Foundation Stone. There was a small sanctuary there and a few men knelt in contemplation, their eyes closed. This was, according to legend, the site of the First Temple of Solomon, which was destroyed by the Babylonians. It was known this was the location of the Second Temple, a structure often written about by various empires. That building was decimated by the Romans and was also the source of many legends and predictions.

None of that interested Wade. His intentions were for a place beneath this exquisite shrine, a region of caves known as the Well of Souls. The Well of Souls was one of the most mysterious locations in the world, a region of caves that may have been part of the, some say mythical, temple of King Solomon. There were reports of Richard Burton and other explorers entering these caverns, but no known exploration team accomplished the feat in many decades. And the religious significance of the shrine itself precluded anyone from mounting a full expedition. Many pilgrims had remarked about how the floor of the rock sounded hollow, but the fabled Well of Souls remained a mystery.

Except to Wade himself, of course. He knew the secret passageways into the tunnel complex and had entered on two occasions. Moving slowly to a smooth outcropping in the stone, he pulled a small brass rod from his robes. Pressing it against the floor at his feet, he watched as the stone appeared to vanish before his eyes. A small opening appeared, and he dropped within, disappearing from the Dome of the Rock instantly. This was the secret method of entering the Well of Souls, a passage created by the ancient builders King Solomon used to create the First Temple. For many years this was a mere passageway to the depths, but at some time it closed and only reopened to the rare few who knew the entry method. Wade learned the mechanism and received the key after fighting the infamous Black Templars years before. Those terrible cultists were attempting to release the plagues of the Egyptians upon all of mankind for their own twisted reasons. But they were gone, their evil forgotten, their libraries of arcane lore safely hidden away on Thunder Island.

The portal vanished as quickly as it appeared, the brass cylinder dropping into Wade's outstretched hand. Then he was in darkness, a gloom so deep and devoid of light he was unable to even see his own body. Pulling out another light globe, he squeezed lightly and was rewarded with a soft illumination. A stone staircase stretched downward before him, a short distance to a wider cavern. Heading down, Wade entered the Well of Souls, a location unseen by most of mankind, a legendary location in the world.

To Wade, this was merely another site of the ancient battle against the enemies of mankind. Since leaving the lost city of the Minoans, his mission was to continue that clash, to defend the world against the lost horrors of the antediluvian ages. This led him to locations such as the Well of Souls constantly, seeking to discover the relics of humanity that could be used to protect them from menaces long forgotten in time.

Fifteen smooth stone steps led him down into a wide but low-ceilinged cave without features. A small stone reliquary was built into the far wall with Aramaic characters barely visible on the surface. The text was long and only slightly visible, but Wade knew this was a memorial, a tribute by the ancient builders to the destroyed First Temple of King Solomon. This was also the locale that led into the true depths of Temple Mount, the site of an ongoing battle since the time of King David of Israel.

According to the writings of the Templars, the warrior King, David of Israel and Judea, discovered a cult of the infamous demon god Moloch hidden in the depths of the earth. The followers of the horrific creature indulged in orgiastic rites that culminated in the sacrifice of babies into a giant metal furnace statue of the horned demon. Many discounted these legends as the truth, since the murder of children was often the accusation leveled against enemies in ancient and modern times. But in this case, the tales were, if possible, a gentler recounting of the horrors of this obscene sect. Upon discovering the truth, David destroyed the cult, scattering them and utilizing these tunnels as a stronghold against the hidden horrors.

His son, King Solomon, was far wiser. He comprehended that mere force of arms would not be enough to prevent the return of the vile, abhorrent followers of this debased faction of baneful beliefs. A positive force was required, a power that would act as a shield against the creatures the devotees of Moloch wished to allow entry into the world. Faith, the wise King realized, was the answer, and he built the First Temple for that, among other reasons. To this day, despite the destruction of the First and Second Temple, the site of Temple Mount had been a beacon of hope to untold numbers of people throughout history. And the attempted destruction of Earth from this location was pushed back.

But the evil still existed; nobody knew how or why, but within the deeper caverns away from Temple Mount, the monsters still held court. Many legends existed as to what kept the horrors clinging in the dark so close to this beacon of hope. Few were credible. But Wade knew the truth: a piece of technology from beyond this world existed in this dark locale. This was one of the legendary secrets known only to the priest of the minotaur in the lost city of Minoans.

Hidden within the depths of the Temple of the Minotaur, beneath the monument to the fabled beast of myth was a chamber containing the metal scrolls of King Minos, God-King of Crete. There, in a lost language known only to the priests, were thousands of secrets of the ancient world, lost in time. Some of the information was scientific, the strange metal of the *Thunderbug*, advanced machinery and technology centuries ahead of the modern world. And other tomes told of the terrible past, when inhuman creatures ruled the Earth and mankind existed for these races as a slave class and food. The three keys and the places mankind hid these terrible items were among the mysteries Wade learned from childhood. And the ancient beings who once ruled humanity were among the most dreaded enigmas he uncovered in his studies. Preventing the return of these antediluvian miscreations was one of the prime reasons Wade returned to the modern world. And sadly, these monstrosities were far from the worst he knew still existed in the shadows of the earth.

Kneeling and examining the altar, Wade placed a finger on the symbols that spelled out the ancient biblical term for God. This word was often interpreted as Yahweh but was a far different pronunciation of the term. Pressing each letter gently, he once again felt the slight indentations of the ancient lock hidden in this religious monument. Wade felt the vibrations as the mechanisms engaged. Then the floor where Wade knelt began to slowly descend into the rock floor, a slow elevator made from the bedrock of the Foundation Stone.

The elevator dropped with steady speed into the earth, moving downward for what felt like an eternity. The tunnel was featureless, made of an odd light stone that was almost frictionless to the touch and exuded a soft yellow light. The descent finally ended at a small platform made of the same mineral, though the surface was more pitted and marked with age and use. No dust was evident, and the air was cool, crisp, and clean.

Wade stood and waited, sensing he was being watched and knowing a hostile movement could mean his fast and painful demise. Hands at his sides, he waited, the seconds stretching into minutes as the silence lengthened.

Finally, a series of shadowy figure flitted across his vision. They were indistinct in the gloom and rarely visible for more than a few seconds. The guards of this keep were examining him, checking to see if he was friend or foe. According to legends, some followers of the Outer Gods attempted to break into this stronghold, desirous of destroying the defenders.

"Identify yourself," a soft voice commanded in an archaic Latin dialect.

Wade slowly raised his hands in a gesture of surrender. "James Clayton Wade. I was granted free entry by His Highness, King Saleim the Fourth."

"Mighty Saleim fell in battle two years, hence," the voice replied. "King Justinian, Ninth of that name, rules now."

Wade nodded once, "I met Justinian, I believe. Was he the Justinian who was Seneschal of the Keep?"

"We do not answer questions, strangers. If the King remembers you, your entry may be allowed. Please wait and do not move forward," the voice stated, hardening slightly.

Wade did not reply, understanding the suspicious nature of these men. They did not offer him food or drink because that would place them under some obligation. Wade knew, without bothering to look, that their weapons were trained on him in the darkness. Without any compunction, these warriors would execute him, and there was little Wade could do to prevent their actions.

After what felt like hours, but was probably less than thirty minutes, a form stepped into the sparse light. He was man of medium height, with dark hair, a thick pointed beard and narrow, suspicious eyes. He was dressed in a mesh metal armor that moved as easily as cloth but was supposedly stronger than steel. A heavy war axe was in his hands and a black metal helmet with no eyeholes hung from his belt.

"The King shall see you," the man stated. "Your hands must be bound hand and foot, and weapons kept at your throat. This is a precaution. If you do not agree, I am to offer you free passage back from whence you came." A group of men in dark cloaks stepped into view. They were all indistinguishable in the murk and they moved with quick, furtive gesticulations which rendered them difficult to pinpoint.

"Agreed," Wade replied and placed his hands behind his back and turned slowly away. Strong hands clapped manacles upon his wrists and ankles, with only a small chain allowing his legs to walk in a slow shuffling fashion. He was gently turned around and a pair of cold metal points touched each side of his neck. Little to no effort would be required to slice his arteries opening, an almost instantaneous death.

"Follow," he was ordered, and Wade took the time to study his companions. There were at least eight, possibly more, and they were dissimilar in every way other than their blank armor and visible weapons. Tall, short, heavy, slim, each man was different in so many ways. But all were dressed alike, dark metal armor, blank faceless helmets, well-used weapons. And they moved with a silent ease, the soft, lithe motions of trained warriors.

Shuffling behind the leader, Wade was led down staircases, through winding corridors and up long ramps for over one hour. Even his keen mind was disoriented by the constant transitions, unable to determine his location in this hidden castle in the depths of Temple Mount. This was intentional; these men were understandably suspicious after almost one thousand years of war.

These combatants were a secret brotherhood known as the Order of the Mount. Formed during the Third Crusade by Sultan Saladin of Egypt, King Richard the Lionhearted, and King Phillip Augustus of France when the infamous assassins attempted to destroy the ancient citadel beneath Temple Mount. All three rulers put aside their religious and political differences and formed a warrior army whose sole mission was to protect the world against the monsters hiding in the shadows. Christians, Muslims, and Jews fought side-by-side, secretly recruiting men around the world to help their never-ending crusade.

Despite their different beliefs, these men lived together, battled side-by-side and even worshipped together, from what Wade had learned over the years. Their common connections formed a sort of quasi-religion based in all three faiths. According to his observations and readings, the Order of the Mount held any form of image based in religion was idolatry, one of the cardinal sins in their mind. It was this belief that led some of the members, who were part of the Templars as well, to spread their beliefs to the outer world. Later, thanks to the help of enemies serving the monsters of the Order, these same Templars were denounced, and many were executed as heretics in Europe.

But the Order continued on, their secret war conducted

without fanfare or even acknowledgment. Their warriors lived and died deep beneath the earth, seeing themselves as the first line of defense against horrors that would drive most men to lose grasp upon their sanity. Where they came from, Wade never knew. He admired their single-minded determination to never yield no matter how desperate the odds. But, in his opinion, their simplistic approach to the powers of good and evil were a little short-sighted. There was a world beyond Temple Mount, one which required committed people who knew of the forgotten terrors of the past. The Order's refusal to protect any other location might keep this place safe, while other dangers rose in the rest of the world. A dangerous gamble, one Wade was not willing to make.

After one hour of twists and turns, spiraling staircases up and down, and ramps, they stopped in a small room, a chamber with small stone cubicles built into the walls. White robes were piled in one of the alcoves, dusty and smelling of mildew and disuse.

"Strip." The leader removed the manacles and leg irons and nodded towards one of the empty cells. The remaining guards hovered in front and behind Wade, their weapons trained on him without pause.

Wade pulled off his clothes, piling them neatly in the stall indicated. He then waited, arms extended as a pair of hands searched his whole body, top to bottom. The frisk was minute and intensive, missing not one inch of his body from the top of his head to the soles of his feet.

"Dress in a robe. Your clothes will be returned after you meet His Majesty, King Justinian." The leader watched Wade with suspicious eyes, his axe still poised for a strike.

"No manacles?" Wade comprehended the suspicious

behavior of the Order. They were always under siege from monsters dwelling in the darkness. This was one of the last bastions in the battle for the Earth and their unwavering attention to duty kept them from losing.

The leader's face clouded with anger, "They will be fastened after you dress. No outsider may enter the hidden chambers of the King without proper precautions."

Wade smiled slightly and dressed in the least ill-smelling robe and allowed the Order's knights to bind him once again. He was led through two rooms and into a square chamber, unadorned except for a stone throne at the rear. A short man, his blonde hair lightening to white sat on chair. He was dressed in the same metallic armor with a battered shotgun across his lap. A huge sword rested near his right arm and he stared at Wade with frank interest.

"You may address the King." The leader turned towards Wade, still holding his axe with clearly murderous intent.

"I will, when he arrives. That's not Justinian. I think your name is Edgar and you used that shotgun to pick a Byakee out of the air when last I was here." Wade nodded at the weapon. The Order's willingness to use modern weapons in their ongoing battle was admirable as well as clever from a strategic standpoint.

A low chuckle sounded from behind Wade and a tall, slender man stepped from the milling guards. He wore a Mauser pistol on his belt and had a pair of curved sabres on his belt. Pulling off his featureless helm, he had long anthracite hair, and a thick dark beard chased his gray and dark brown skin. His smile was broad, and he appeared very amused by the events.

"I did warn you, my friend." Justinian took the throne from Edgar, who stood at the King's side. "This one is no average pilgrim. Sir Wade, I present you Sir Moshe, my captain of the guards."

"The security of all is my job, Majesty." Moshe addressed the King and ignored Wade.

"Your procedures are outdated." Wade looked at Moshe with some amusement. "We are two levels below where I entered. And there's a lockpick kit and small knife beneath a false scar on my lower back."

Moshe's mouth opened to protest and was rendered silent as Wade handed the security captain the arm manacles. Wade also handed the man the small knife and the lock pick kit and waited calmly as the manacles were affixed again.

"Enough," Justinian waved Moshe's protests aside, "Security is important, all-important. But we also must remember we serve mankind. Wade came to us as a pilgrim. We will trust your security and listen to the man without anger or fear in our hearts."

"Thank you." Wade gave the King a sketch of a bow. "I need to make sure the Heart of Ahriman is safe. A follower of the ancient rulers of the Earth seeks to awaken their tombs. The Heart is a piece of the key."

"No!" Moshe stepped closer to Wade, his face filled with anger and his gun raised and ready. "None may see the Heart of Ahriman! It is a sacred treasure. You should not even know it exists."

"James Clayton Wade saved the Heart for us once." Justinian stepped between his captain and Thunder Jim. "Saleim trusted this man. I will do so as well."

"Very well," Moshe lowered his weapon, "The security will stay in place. I viewed it myself through the door last week. The Heart still rests in the alcove."

"We will all check." Justinian waved the guards to proceed

and stepped next to Wade. "You fought this servant of the ancients?

Wade nodded, "He had a Servitor at his side. Very dangerous."

"I thought they were extinct." Moshe was at Wade's other side, still watching him with open suspicion.

"As did I." Wade's movements were slow because of the leg irons and manacles, but he still tried to keep up with the King and captain. "Then one walked through fire and changed from soft to hard before my eyes."

Justinian shrugged. "Then we will find a means of destroying the last one. Our ancestors managed the feat. Are we lesser men than those before us? I think not."

Wade had nothing further to add, so he merely followed the knights into the depths of the keep. The walls were stone, smooth from constant use and appeared to be carved out of the stones of the earth and into the form of an ancient castle. Many stone and metal doors and gates were visible, providing each area with multiple defenses, both visible and unseen. Men were occasionally in view, all dressed for war and in possession of weapons that ranged from Greek and Roman soldiers to the most modern armaments of the present age. The Order was an army, a balanced one with each man working with the weapons that best suited their mind, body, and skills.

They arrived at one of the deepest subbasements a short time later. A massive door made of rune-sketched steel was set in a wall at least three stories high. Wade was turned around so his back was to the door as a series of locks were disengaged. A moment later he was turned and led into a long, empty chamber with a white stone altar at the far end. Upon the platform rested a jewel slightly larger than a man's fist and made of a deep red stone. The gem pulsed with a red fire, a powerful glow that seemed to emanate from within the depths of the multitude of glittering facets.

Wade sniffed the air once, frowned and looked at Edgar. "Please fire your gun at the Heart."

"It will ricochet!" Moshe stepped forward, looking suspicious again.

Wade rolled his eyes and shook his head. "Nuts to that! Place me in front of the door and fire the gun under my arm. Keep behind the wall. Only I will be in danger."

Justinian raised a hand to prevent any protests. "Fire the gun now, Sir Edgar. My orders."

Edgar stepped past everyone and fired the gun once. A loud blast filled the air, partially deafening all present. The Heart of Ahriman shattered in an explosion of scintillating slivers, a crimson spray covering the wall and floor.

"The Heart was stolen." Wade nodded towards the destruction. "No Earth-created weapon could pierce a device so potent."

"How?" Moshe looked crazed in his question, his hands gripping his beloved axe with white knuckled fury.

Wade studied the room and turned back to the knights and their king. "Fire your weapons at the altar and start backing to the door."

"Do as he orders." Justinian drew his sidearm and fired in one motion. The bullet struck the altar and passed through to the rear wall.

"Fire!" Moshe pulled an automatic pistol seemingly from nowhere and began shooting his gun at the altar. Edgar joined in, his shotgun barking as he backed towards the door. Soon all of the knights were firing their guns, the echoes earsplitting for all present or nearby.

The altar seemed unaffected by the gunfire, with each lead slug passing through and striking the wall behind the platform. No chips of stone flew about the chamber, no blemishes appeared on the face of the tabernacle which once contained the Heart of Ahriman. Finally Justinian held up a hand and the gunfire ended instantly.

"What is the cause of this?" The King holstered his gun and pulled out his well-used blades. The weapons glinted in the soft light of the room, the razor edges of the swords shining.

"That," Wade nodded towards the altar, "is a Servitor. We need to destroy it now. Otherwise this keep is not safe."

The altar suddenly rose up, forming a vaguely human shape. The glutinous, miry, gelatinous flesh appeared to writhe as it formed, as if the very tissue of the creature was an unstable mass. A pair of gruesome red eyes emerged from the location where there should be a face and a maw filled with enormous serrated teeth appeared before their horrified eyes. A pair of ropy six-fingered hands appeared at the end of mucilaginous, elongated tendrils that appeared to be something akin to arms.

"Another Servitor?" Justinian looked surprised as he reloaded his revolver.

Wade shook his head, "The same one. They can divide. One being, two places. But it weakens their strength."

A raspy cough emerged from the gaping gob of the Servitor. It appeared to be the brute's version of a laugh of derision. "Powerful enough to fool your mammalian eyes, mortal. More than enough to destroy you and all who reside here with ease."

"I doubt that." Wade stepped forward and raised his flame gun. He fired a long burst at the Servitor, causing the ancient miscreation to rear back and shrink inward.

"Where did you get that weapon?" Moshe looked at Wade with angry accusing eyes.

"I palmed it when you had me dress in this stinking robe." Wade fired a second blast and nodded towards the Servitor, "The thing is hardening, becoming immune to my fire. Only a few seconds now."

"We have an answer for that difficulty." Justinian smiled as a pair of men appeared, toting several large metal boxes. The crates where thrown open and even Wade's calm gaze widened in some surprise.

"That's an M2 Browning .50 caliber machine gun. Your Order is up-to-date in armaments." Wade shook his head. "I don't recognize the other but I can guess. I'll keep the Servitor busy while you set up."

Justinian was about to protest, but Wade bounded into the room. He decided to be slightly theatrical about his actions, wishing to annoy the monster. He performed several backwards and forward flips, resembling a pinwheel more than a human man. The ancient fighting arts of the lost city of Minoans were based in the arts of the Cretan's traditional bull dancing ceremonies. The ceremony involved leaping and performing acrobatics while the massive animal attempted to gore the warrior. The height of the rite was where the young gymnast would pluck ribbons from the maddened bull's horns without being harmed. Wade underwent these observances and emerged victorious multiple times by age 11, younger than any in history. He then was taken, as was his right and honor, to be trained in the many ancient fighting arts recorded by the Temple of the Minotaur. The temple, old by the time the pyramids where being built, was the last stronghold of this knowledge in the world.

"I recognize that movement." The Servitor emerged from the flames, body moving stiffly. The being's form was no-longer the oozy mass as before, but now a hardened gray-skinned stone, a moving statue. "You follow the traitor lord Minos, one of the nine ancient rebels against the masters!"

Wade laughed, knowing this would madden his opponent. Servitors were infamous for their lack of comprehension of humor. "He and the others weren't rebels."

The Servitor charged forward, heavy pole-like legs stomping the ground as it moved, "Yes they were! They rebelled against their rightful lord. That makes them traitors!"

Wade dove backwards and landed on his hands, backing up several steps in this ludicrous position. "Since they won, that makes them liberators against the ancient, disgusting monsters who enslaved the earth. Heroes, unlike the pathetic, terrified, extinct demons your kind once served."

The Servitor grew two additional legs and surged forward with uncanny speed and grace. Wade ran away, still using his hands in place of his feet, moving with the swiftness of an Olympic runner. The effect was comic and bizarre, with Justinian and several members of the Order tittering from the distant doorway.

"The Masters will return! Their overseer brings the three keys to the last tomb of their kind! They will awaken and take back control of all! And then the way will be opened. Aforgomon is the key, Aforgomon is the guardian of the gate. Aforgomon knows the ways of the Old Ones and will open the paths. They will break through again and remake the world in the image!" The Servitor's chant was a barely human croak, a terrible cacophony that caused even the powerful men of the Order to wince.

Wade appeared oblivious to the statements of the creature.

He vaulted to his feet, stood still and then suddenly dove forward, sliding like a professional baseball player through the running legs of the Servitor. As the monster spun in place and moved to follow, he backflipped over the horror's form and took off running backwards. The Servitor howled at the open mockery, growing four more legs and running with greater speed. It now resembled a hideous arachnid, a nightmarish insectoid demon of white alluvium tissue.

"Wade! Now!" Justinian's voice was calm despite the strong word of command, a man used to barking orders under the most dangerous of circumstances.

Wade rolled out, pressing his back against the wall closest to the doorway. A heartbeat later, the enormous machine gun began to fire. A long tongue of flame emerged from the steel barrel as the knights of the Orders fired one of the most powerful infantry weapons on Earth. Created to destroy humans, light armored vehicles or light fortifications, this gun was designed as one of the most dangerous tools or warfare in the history of mankind. Had Joshua Chamberlain possessed even one of these devices at Little Round Top or Pickett's Charge, the Battle of Gettysburg would have been ended in mere seconds. The sheer destructive power of these massive bullets would tear a man in two pieces.

But not a Servitor. The demonic monster was thrown back by the volume of shots, the intensity even causing the viscid protoplasm of the creature to be thrown backwards. But the mire that was the Servitor's composition slowly returned to itself, reforming before their eyes.

The gunshots abruptly cut off and Justinian's head peeked around the corner. He waved for Wade to step outside the chamber, which the adventurer did without demur. A pair of men crouched in the large doorway, long metal tubes resting across their shoulders. Wade stepped aside and covered his ears as Justinian growled a command. Both knights fired, the small rockets on the end of the tubes shooting into the room and detonated with earth shattering explosions that tossed both men backwards. The huge door was then slammed shut, locking mechanisms engaging with loud clicks.

"I doubt that can destroy a Servitor. They were said to be nearly impossible to destroy." Wade looked at Justinian but found the man to be smiling.

"That is unimportant. Do you believe our Keep was never infiltrated prior to this day? Our battle dates back millennia, we are merely the latest men to take up arms against the darkness. This enclosure will be sealed and warded, closed off for eternity. Another place for the Heart will be carved from the living rock. We must find the means the Servitor entered and stole the Heart of Ahriman." Justinian holstered his weapon, speaking loudly because of the deafening noise of the weapons.

Wade studied the titanic door and tapped the sliding viewing window. "The creature slid through this small port. They are adaptive. This made them a danger in ancient days. But I believe I know how to defeat them, thanks to this small battle."

Justinian smiled and nodded. "You remind me of an American who lived with us for a time. A giant American man with a magnificent mind."

"I'll take that as a compliment. Unfortunately, the current situation is very bad. Tristan Twilight and the Servitor probably possess all three pieces of the key to the Tombs of the Ancients. I have no knowledge of the location of that place. It's lost in time." Wade looked angry, but very determined.

"Think not of the jewel." Justinian was still smiling as the members of the Order put away their weapons. "Think of your enemy. What type of a man is this Twilight?"

"Vainglorious, sadistic, foolish, arrogant, cruel, and angry. He wishes to make people his slaves." Wade frowned in thought. Then a terrible thought struck him...the Servitor knew of his battle in the depths of Temple Mount. This meant that the Servitor at the side of Twilight possessed that information.

"I need to get back to the airport, immediately." Wade looked at the King, the intensity of his concern evident to all present.

"It shall be done. We will take you to a tunnel that will lead you within one hundred yards of that location." Justinian looked to Moshe, who saluted in response. "May your way be blessed, James Clayton Wade. Please return the Heart of Ahriman to us for protection. We will take other precautions to protect the device from the hands of outsiders."

"My thanks," Wade called back and followed Moshe and his men into the depths of the keep. He was impatient to leave the keep of the Order but knew their security procedures would not allow him a fast egress.

Forty minutes later, Wade ran through the airport. The *Thunderbug* was out of sight, hidden in a distant corner of the British military's auspices. Wade bounded along, his movements quick but controlled, his hand gripping a flamer.

There was no need. The *Thunderbug's* hatch was wide open. This was what he feared, that Twilight's anger would lead him to attack Wade's aides. Gripping his flame gun tight, Wade carefully stepped into the marvel of advanced aerodynamic science. He was greeted by silence, and an empty cockpit. Searching carefully, he found nothing missing, all the instruments untouched.

There was a note pinned to the main console, written in a slashing script that resembled the slashes of a knife in the hands of a crazed killer. It took some time to decipher, but finally Wade was able to make out the letter.

"They call you Thunder Jim. I call you sad and weak. You robbed me of my servants, I shall take yours in recompense. They will exist as my slaves. When the masters return, I will kill them before your eyes and force you to kill yourself slowly. Live in pain and fear, Thunder Jim Wade. Your days are numbered!

Tristan Twilight, Overseer of Mankind

Wade frowned, wondering briefly why Twilight didn't steal the *Thunderbug* as well. But the answer was simple to realize after a moment's contemplation. Twilight could maintain absolute control of Lise, Dirk and Red; he was that powerful. But he was unskilled in flying a plane, especially one as complex as the *Thunderbug*. Wade's aides, if allowed enough free-will to fly the amazing airship, would immediately rebel and attempt to kill Twilight and the Servitor. As for the Servitor, they were dangerous and terrible killers, but not renowned for their high intelligence.

In kidnapping away his aides, Twilight made an error. Wade and his aides all wore radio transmitters which doubled as tracking devices. Hitting several switches, Wade tuned into their frequencies and a moment later located their signal. They were heading east at a little below 200 miles per hour. That was a decent pace for most planes and well-below half the speed of the *Thunderbug*.

Wade frowned, disliking the idea of Lise, Dirk, and Red

under the power of Twilight. But this vain assault by Twilight could lead to the location of the secret tomb. Therefore Wade was forced to make the horrible choice to leave his closest friends in the hands of the madman. That way he could eliminate an ancient evil from the world, once and for all. Wade knew he would never forgive himself for this choice.

Resigned to his decision, Wade radioed ahead to his other agents, ordering the items he would require taking on a Servitor. That monster, despite being horrifically lethal, was the lesser danger. The Servitor's dark master was the stuff of nightmares, creatures so terrible their race was wiped from all history for fear their heinous legacy might return.

"The Ancient Worms shall not rise again," Wade whispered to himself, suppressing a shudder of horror.

⚡

"**I** STILL FAIL to comprehend your reason for keeping these mammals alive." The Servitor's voice was a harsh rasp, a loathsome bass profundo that could not have emerged from human organs.

Twilight giggled and looked over at Lise, Dirk, and Red as they crouched in the corner of the cargo hold. For his pleasure, they were behaving like the ghouls he used as servants earlier, debased subhumans lacking in even the slightest dignity. Perhaps he would make them dance like little children later. Their continued humiliation was a pleasure he would soon find dull, but for now Twilight would enjoy the degradation of these strong spirits.

"First, we need servants to carry our goods to the tomb of the masters. More importantly because I enjoy making them serve me." Twilight stared across the cargo hold at the large crate containing the three keys. These items were his means to achieving his destiny to be a king of legend.

The Servitor released a bizarre cacophony of sounds, which Twilight realized was this monster's version of a laugh. "Mammals, reptiles, you all are alike. Every overseer behaves such."

"What do you mean by that? I listened to your words and we took the Heart before Wade. The rest only makes sense!" Twilight said, his voice a low hiss. He snapped his fingers and Dirk shuffled to his side, crouching down on hands and knees. Tristan stretched his legs out, using the formerly dapper soldier-of-fortune as a mere footrest.

The Servitor's alien red eyes stared down at Twilight, no expression readable in the creature's inhuman visage. "When the ancient masters arrived from the stars, three races served as their slaves. The lizards, who styled themselves as dragon kings, the snakes, also called by some the serpent men, and your races of mammals. Each were controlled by overseers. They took titles such King Balor or Lord Ymir, but in the end they were merely servants of the masters. And all the overseers behaved as you do. They reveled in their control of the lesser, debasing their kind for pleasure. And each were tossed down by their own kind. It is a cycle we Servitors observed. Just as the shoggoths destroyed the Elder Ones in the time before the masters took this world."

"The cycle ends now." Twilight stared at the Servitor with naked disgust. His powers did not affect this creature, but one day he would find its weakness. Then he would make it pay for comparing him to the fools of the past.

"Does it? I doubt your species is capable of such growth. Only the masters are perfect," the Servitor intoned.

"Perfect? Yes, of course. They are ever so wondrous and

amazing." Twilight didn't hide his sarcasm, knowing the monster was not capable of comprehending that form of communication. He settled back in his seat, dreaming of his future as the king of all.

⚡

TRACKING HIS AIDES to the Kuruk Tagh region of the Gobi desert was a surprise; Wade never imagined the ancient tomb was hidden within such desolation. When he imagined the tombs of antediluvian monstrosities such as the Ancient Worms, his mind pictured lost cities in the heart of the Earth. Or beneath burial grounds or sacred locations such as the Sphinx of Egypt or the lost cities of Mongolia. A site of bleak, forlorn, atrophied lands, a mountain region wasted by time to near nothingness seemed an unlikely place for the formerly great races. Wade realized this was a failing on his part, a gap in his understanding. If he and his aides survived this encounter, his searches would grow deeper and more detailed, looking into possibilities he formerly failed to study.

Preparing for over a week for this battle, Wade rocketed across the deepest portion of the desert. Twilight's inability to pilot a plane was a difficulty that slowed their progress. His powers didn't allow him to control the pilot and none would be crazy enough to risk their lives in the Gobi. Twilight's caravan made fast time, covering the ground with impressive speed. Compared to the *Thunderbug*, they were moving in slow motion.

Landing near the hillock, Wade spotted five figures heading for the north side of the ridge. Though covered in robes, Thunder Jim spotted the huge Red and the whipcord thin Dirk lugging a large crate towards the east side. One figure stopped to stare at the *Thunderbug* and then turned to the others. The party continued towards this formerly great mountain, their pace slightly faster.

Wade was ready for this retreat. The *Thunderbug* roared to life again, the powerful treads driving through the Gobi Desert almost as fast on the ground as it was in the skies. Twilight's party ducked into the ridge, a hidden path that Wade spotted, the entire reason he landed rather than remaining in the air.

Grabbing a large backpack, Wade was out of the *Thunderbug* and on the party's heels in seconds. He ignored the choking dust, the harsh, harrowing heat. Nothing mattered but protecting the world and rescuing his aides. He spotted the entry; a large boulder, formerly blocking a deep, dark cave mouth, now lay nearby. Dust and sand filled the air, thrown up by the motion of the enormous rock. Holding his breath and closing his eyes, Wade stepped into the depths of the Earth, the entryway to the tomb of the Ancient Worms.

Opening his eyes when the temperature dropped slightly, Wade's eyes were immediately adjusted to the light. He was standing in a creaseless cavern, the surfaces resembling glass more than rock. There were legends that these minerals emerged from space, that they were the remnants of the craft which brought the Ancient Worms to the Earth. Others held they created their cities and homes by science so advanced, it was beyond the dreams of mankind. Either way, Wade knew he was in the right place.

Following the walkway, he suddenly felt a fast movement of air. Ducking quickly to the side, Wade's keen vision spotted a sliver of silver shooting past where he once stood. A throwing knife, the signature weapon of Dirk. Twilight wisely sent the slender blade expert against Wade, knowing the man was one of the deadliest warriors on the planet.

A second knife appeared, thrown exactly where Wade now stood, forcing the adventurer to drop to his knees. The blade sliced across the edge of Wade's ear, a small spray of blood hitting the glassine wall and floor. Running forward, he batted aside a third blade, cutting his hand but closing on Dirk.

But Dirk wasn't standing still; he pulled out a pair of knives, dropped into a low crouch and smiled. If he couldn't throw his blades, there was nothing Dirk liked better than a knife fight. Wade stopped, unwilling to pull out his own dagger and risk killing one of his closest friends. This made the battle all the more dangerous. Dirk, under the control of Twilight's command, would not be so willing to hold back.

But then Wade smiled, realizing that Twilight did not possess Dirk's skills in a fight. Oh, he could order the slender killer to throw his blades, which Dirk would do with consummate expertise. But a prolonged knife fight, using blades and hand-to-hand combat? No. Dirk was hampered by his controller, a dangerous psychic with little understanding of weapons.

Dropping both hands to his side, Wade twisted his face into a look of sadness. "I could never attack you, Dirk."

Dirk's face seemed to crease in a cruel smile and he raised a knife high, stepping forward and bringing the keen blade downward to Wade's heart. This theatrical attack proved Dirk was under Twilight's control. Blade experts like Dirk always stabbed up under the rib cage or in their enemy's sides or neck.

Stepping forward, Wade blocked Dirk's stabbing hand with a raised arm. Grabbing the wrist in an iron grip, he kicked Dirk's other arm, sending the second knife clattering to the ground. Dirk grunted in pain and reached into his robes, pulling out another blade. Wade shifted closer and hit Dirk's temple with the edge of his hand. Wade then swept his aide to the ground and punched him in the jaw, knocking his aide out. The thin soldier-of-fortune would be well soon enough, but for now he was out-of-commission.

Moving deeper into the tunnels, Wade was unsurprised to spot Red's bulk in the distance. Upon realizing Dirk was unconscious or dead, Twilight sent the next of Wade's aide to slow him down. The giant Red was a formidable opponent, a massive man with massive, terrible strength. But Wade didn't have time to waste defeating his friend. This would need to be performed quickly, without injuring Red badly.

Wade ran forward and was gratified to see Red charging his way, looking more like a bull than a man. When they were a short distance apart, Wade stopped and dropped to his knees and took Red's legs out from under him. The giant, unable to stop, flew and crashed to the cavern floor, his wind knocked out, momentarily stunned. Wade leaped onto Red's back and depressed a series of nerves at the base of his aide's giant neck. Red slumped to the ground, unconscious.

Rising, Wade walked further into the tunnel, turning a corner and believing he was close to the tomb. Would Twilight send the Servitor or Lise against him now? The question was moot as he spotted the Servitor heading his way, the creature's bizarre form moving with inhuman grace.

"You are to die. The ancient masters will return in moments and take back this world in the name of Aforgomon. Aforgomon is the key, Aforgomon is the guardian of the gate. Aforgomon knows the ways of the Old Ones and will open the paths. They will break through again and remake the world in the image!" The Servitor's recitation was performed in the same inhuman intonations Wade heard in the vaults of Temple Mount.

"Nuts to that," Wade replied and reached into his backpack. He pulled out a heavy metal tube with a nozzle on the end and a thick rubber handle. Turning the switch on the top, he pulled the trigger and a stream of hot liquid metal flew out. The metal struck the Servitor, covering the creature in seconds and emptying the tank.

"This will not stop me." The Servitor's voice was muffled as the silver liquid metal covered its form.

Thunder Jim reached into the other side of the backpack and pulled out an identical nozzle and fired. A smoky streak of liquid fired out, filling the room with a harsh, painful chill. Wade took several steps back and dropped the back pack to the ground. It opened slightly, revealing a network of wires, dials, and wheels, a complex set of machinery.

Where there was once the white, fluid muck that was the substance of a Servitor, there stood a silver-gray statue. Curls of steam rose off the body and an unpleasant frigid chill emerged from the body.

"Liquid metal mixed with liquid nitrogen. Freezing your unstable molecules. It might not destroy you, but you won't be bothering anyone for a few hundred centuries." Wade carefully stepped around the now frozen Servitor. It wasn't easy to transport such dangerous chemicals, but he had designed a method over the last week.

Leaving the Servitor behind, Wade stepped into a small boxlike room with glowing walls, a huge jewel on the floor. Twilight and Lise were standing near the glowing gem, the huge crate behind them. Wade quickly realized that in attempting to slow him down, Twilight and Lise were forced to slowly pull the box to this room.

The Heart of Ahriman was in Twilight's hand and Lise held the Shining Trapezohedron. As Wade stepped into view, they placed these two ancient objects onto the glowing jewel, causing the gem to glow brighter. Both ignored Wade and turned back to the box, reaching inside.

"Stop. Right now." Wade stepped into view and pulled out his flame gun.

Twilight turned his direction, smiling. "You got past the Servitor? I'm impressed. I will make you my first slave when I'm overseer of this world. The masters promised my powers would be strong enough to control all."

Wade shook his head. "You think an overseer is a king? I thought you were smarter than that."

Twilight's eyes narrowed. "What are you saying? You know you can't stop me. My powers are enough to hold you off while your aide presents the Statue of Tsathoggua to the masters."

"An overseer is a slave who is in charge of his fellow slaves. He can call himself a king, god or whatever, the Ancient Worms didn't care. The overseers were the foremen to make sure the slaves produced enough lives for sacrifice and feeding. Nothing more. If you fail, they eat you or sacrifice you to the Outer Gods. The being known as Aforgomon has no interest in humanity. The Ancient Worms seek to control this world in Aforgomon's name and remake all life in a manner more pleasing for that Outer God. Humans are not part of the equation," Wade explained, smiling. He was exaggerating, but only slightly. Twilight's vanity was his weakness and Wade wasn't above using this as a weapon.

"You're lying!" Twilight snarled and turned towards a blank wall. "He's lying! Tell me! I have done as you demanded.

The keys are here and will awaken your people. But am I nothing more than another peon beneath you?"

The wall slid aside, and a large rectangular gem appeared before their eyes. The jewel was multifaceted, pale yellow in color and appeared to pulse with a gold energy. The top slid aside, and a creature slithered into view. Four feet high with sickly gray-green skin which was covered in a thick layer of oozing yellow mucus. The body slithered out of the crystalline sarcophagus, revealing a black metallic belt covered in gems of many colors around the monstrosity's mid-section.

"You wished to be a king. That is what many overseers called themselves in the past," the Ancient Worm answered in their minds. "You may play with your kind all you wish. You mammals lead very unimportant, short lives. Your duties are simple: provide more lives for sacrifice or experiment."

Wade chuckled and shook his head. "They are making you a farmer. You always wanted to be a common man, didn't you Twilight?"

"No! That is not acceptable! I am Tristan Twilight, I shall be master of all life, God King of the Earth!" Twilight's hands rose dramatically as he snarled at the Ancient Worm.

"You are Arthur Jones," the Ancient Worm replied. "Your grandfather was the fourth son of a lesser nobleman of your species. Your bloodline is one of many that served us when we ruled. If you will not comply, we shall find others."

Twilight's face twisted with rage and he stared at the Ancient Worm. There was a feeling of tension in the air as he brought his powers to bear. Nothing happened for a full minute. Nothing seemed to move.

"You seek to use powers we granted you against us? Your mammalian mind can't begin to grasp the powers we possess. But you are of no use to us," the Ancient Worm intoned as a red gem upon the creature's back flared.

Suddenly Twilight's body burst into flames. He shrieked in agony and fled up the cavern tunnel, his wails of agony echoing as he vanished from view. Lise immediately slumped, the magus's control of her mind vanished.

"Run," Wade told her, pushing her towards the exit. He fired his flame gun at the Ancient Worm, knowing this weapon was of no use in this battle. But it was a brief distraction.

Lise looked at the horrific creature slithering forward, nodded, and ran from sight. The echo of her feet soon could not be heard, even by Wade's keen senses.

Releasing the trigger, Wade was unsurprised to find the ancient worm was untouched by the fire. An orange jewel was glowing upon its belt, fading out as the flames vanished. But at least his aides were away from this terrible relic of an ancient dreadful time.

"Place the Statue of Tsathoggua on the platform. You will be rewarded, mammal." The Ancient Worm slithered closer as it spoke in Wade's mind.

"Never," Wade replied, stepping away from the glowing gem.

A blue light flared on the ancient worm's belt. "Then you shall discover the agonies your primitive nervous system can experience. And you shall comply."

A pain like a knife stabbing in his brain struck Wade, causing him to groan and drop to his knees. He found he was on his stomach, not even remembering falling. Blood fell from his nose and ears and his vision was blurred, twisting and filling him with nausea. The torment grew by each second and a soft voice entered his mind once again.

"Agree to do as you were ordered. Agree and the pain will

end."

Wade forced his head upward and opened his nearly blind eyes, "No," he gasped.

It was then that he spotted a knife blade sticking out of the Ancient Worm's side. The pain in Wade's body slackened and a second knife appeared next to the first. The Worm reared back and the orange light appeared again, causing a third knife to bounce off an invisible wall.

"Lise, grab the statue." Red stepped into view, placing Wade's backpack at his feet.

The blue gem on the Ancient Worm's back began to glow as the orange light faded. Dirk appeared next to Red, another knife in hand. He threw it at the Ancient Worm, the blade sinking deep into the soft flesh of the alien being. The orange light glowed again, causing another blade to bounce away and the blue light to vanish. Lise stepped past Wade, her face registering the horror as she grabbed the yellow stone idol of a being that resembled a terrifying combination of a bat, sloth and a toad. Lise strained to move the small object, lugging it as Dirk continued to pepper the Ancient Worm with his collection of blades. None struck the creature, but it appeared unable to attack any further.

Lise vanished from view and Red moved next to Wade. He paused to scoop up the Heart of Ahriman and the Shining Trapezohedron in one huge hand and Wade in the other. Lise reappeared just as Red stepped out of the room, pulling her flame gun out and firing it at the ancient worm.

"Let's go, kid," Dirk stated, pulling out his flame gun and adding to the fire. They began to back out, cutting off the fire when they turned to run.

As they all turned the corner, there was a low banging sounded, a small explosion back near the room the Ancient

Worm held sway. Helping Wade stand, Red gave his leader a brief smile.

"I wired your thingamajig in the pack to blow. It won't be even as much as a stick of dynamite, but it will give us a few seconds to get out of this crazy place," Red explained, watching Wade carefully.

Wade coughed and began to walk forward, his movements jerky and uncoordinated. He would need some time to rest and recover, possibly a month on Thunder Island mediating. But this time, he would show his secret base to his aides; they deserved to know the secret after this terrible experience. "How did you figure out how to hurt the Ancient Worm?" he gasped out.

"It was simple, boss," Dirk said, taking the Heart of Ahriman from Red so the giant could help Thunder Jim walk. "What would a caveman do if facing something trying to kill him? Run away or hit it with a stick."

Lise continued the thought. "It's all we could think to do. But that doesn't stop those monsters from existing. You could just feel how evil they were, so wrong!"

"That is why I brought several bombs of my own design. I intend to seal these caves and the surrounding ridge. The Ancient Worms might not age, but they won't be returning anytime soon. Then we need to find safe places for these three artifacts," Wade explained, grateful he resisted the Ancient Worm's orders. The one who placed these keys in place was the first sacrifice to the Outer Gods.

I'm taking you to Thunder Island for rest and recovery. There I can teach you our real work for this world, Wade thought as his three aides began dividing the labor of planting the explosives quickly in case the Ancient Worm they met was coming behind them.

The cavern and all traces of the path vanished after a series of carefully planned explosions. After a brief search for other corridors, the team left with Dirk piloting the *Thunderbug*. Hours later it occurred to Lise they forgot something.

"What ever happened to Tristan Twilight?" she asked, and none could supply an answer.

⚡

MONTHS LATER A man walked from the desert, his face and body covered in a tattered desert robe. "Kneel before me. I am your salvation, I am your master and I will lead you to glory," the man croaked, his voice a bare whisper.

The people, a simple desert tribe in a small town on the edge of the Gobi, found themselves complying, not knowing why. They pressed their faces into the dust, unable to look at their new prophet.

"Who are you?" the headman asked, unable to lift his head.

"I am the Black Monk, the King of the Earth, and all shall obey my commands," the man formerly known as Tristan Twilight rasped. He would find more followers and then Thunder Jim Wade and his followers would be the first to fall as he took over the earth. Then the way would be paved for the Outer Gods. The Servitor told him much of the ways of the universe and he remembered the truth. *Aforgomon is the key, Aforgomon is the guardian of the gate. Aforgomon knows the ways of the Old Ones and will open the paths. They will break through again and remake the world in the image!* he thought to himself and began to chuckle.

ABOUT THE AUTHOR

Frank Schildiner is a martial arts instructor at Amorosi's Mixed Martial Arts in New Jersey. He is the writer of the novels, THE QUEST OF FRANKENSTEIN, THE TRIUMPH OF FRANKENSTEIN, NAPOLEON'S VAMPIRE HUNTERS, THE DEVIL PLAGUE OF NAPLES, and the forthcoming SATANIC GANGS OF NEW YORK. Frank is a regular contributor to the fictional series TALES OF THE SHADOWMEN and has been published in THE JOY OF JOE, THE NEW ADVENTURES OF THUNDER JIM WADE, SECRET AGENT X Volumes 3, 4, 5, 6, THE LONE RANGER AND TONTO: FRONTIER JUSTICE, and THE AVENGER: THE JUSTICE FILES. He resides in New Jersey with his wife Gail who is his top supporter and two cats who are indifferent on the subject.

13950336R00058

Made in the USA
Lexington, KY
03 November 2018